MW01699974

Tales Out Of Time

The Allure of the Beloved

ROBERT J. ROSENTHAL, PH.D.

DORRANCE
PUBLISHING CO
EST. 1920
PITTSBURGH, PENNSYLVANIA 15238

The contents of this work, including, but not limited to, the accuracy of events, people, and places depicted; opinions expressed; permission to use previously published materials included; and any advice given or actions advocated are solely the responsibility of the author, who assumes all liability for said work and indemnifies the publisher against any claims stemming from publication of the work.

All Rights Reserved
Copyright © 2021 by Robert J. Rosenthal, Ph. D.

No part of this book may be reproduced or transmitted, downloaded, distributed, reverse engineered, or stored in or introduced into any information storage and retrieval system, in any form or by any means, including photocopying and recording, whether electronic or mechanical, now known or hereinafter invented without permission in writing from the publisher.

Dorrance Publishing Co
585 Alpha Drive
Pittsburgh, PA 15238
Visit our website at *www.dorrancebookstore.com*

ISBN: 978-1-6376-4388-4
EISBN: 978-1-6376-4422-5

Contents

Foreword

Dear Reader: This is a collection of fifteen short stories, having a common style and theme. The first section was mainly written in 1977-78, consisting of quite brief tales about a variety of responses to the lure of an ideal beloved. The second set is three longer, more elaborated, stories on the same theme. Those were written after my retirement (as a professor of philosophy) in 2014. The final set is three tales about the relation between an emperor and a servant who designs and maintains a contemplative garden for the emperor. All have a "long ago and far away" tone and style, but deal with quite universal human concerns and situations. I hope that you enjoy them and find them worthy of your reflection.

Dedication

The first and primary reader of these tales has been my wife, Vicki Lynn Jenkins, to whom I dedicate this anthology. She is the true Beloved of my life, the source, center and companion of my journey in this world.

Robert Rosenthal
February, 2021

Acknowledgements

I have especially benefitted from the comments and support of two other people: colleague and friend Dr. James Ferguson, emeritus Professor of English, Hanover College, and Frederick Longan, a dear friend for over 60 years

The Forest Hermit

Long ago, when such things still happened, there was a hermit who lived deep in a forest. He was old, or seemed old; though, living by the seasons, he did not keep the years. He had lived alone for a long time. The farmers in that land knew of him, and the hunters sometimes saw him on their rare trips into the center of the forest.

Some said he had been a prince who gave up all claim to his kingdom to seek something holy among the ancient silent trees. Others said he had never been young, that he had grown out of a twisted oak burl, already a knotted old man. He lived in the trees; the animals talked to him; he hibernated through the winter. The sturdy peasants told such stories to each other, guessing at what they could not understand and were afraid to discover. But they did not fear that he would harm them.

Once each year two hunters carried jugs far into the forest to get the cold pure water that flowed from the hermit's spring. This water made the base for many cures prepared by aged women of that region. The hunters would stay close to each other, moving silently in the heavy stillness of the trees. Each moment they looked at each other to keep their bond, marveling at how they became pale golden forms in the muted light that filtered through the lofty leaves.

When they heard the faint laughter of the spring, they would smile and move more surely toward the lively sound. The spring sparkled and splashed from the mossy mouth of a small cave, falling in a smooth curve over the lip of a granite slab into a cup of broken rock, disappearing underground with a sound like the small voices of sprites.

The hunters said it was at these times, filling their jugs under the transparent arc of icy water, that they sometimes saw him or sensed him standing in the darkness of the tall trees, his large still eyes like those of an owl watching them. They would hurry to finish, fearful that he might approach them, afraid of what his voice would do to them after so much silence in the solitude of this still place. Without looking where they knew he stood, the hunters would turn back to the path.

It was a sacred spring. The hermit had felt that when he first found it. He had refreshed himself with its waters and slept close to it, letting its hidden voices carry his thoughts into the earth. In the beginning he had talked to himself and to the world around him: but long ago he had fallen silent, letting the spring be his perpetual voice.

Its flow was so constant that from one year to another it would not alter its litany. Pressing up from a great depth, the spring did not show the impact of droughts or rainy seasons, except with a long delay. Then he would hear the tone sink or rise, with new lamentations or supplications or psalms of praise.

It was in such a rare season, when the surface world was already budding and blooming (while the spring kept repeating its imploring words, weary with recollections of rainless seasons long past) that he sensed there would be a turning, a new antiphon. The moon glowed through the fringed green branches, reborn, its soft white light falling on the low glinting water. He felt, before he heard, the first new stirring: a sudden gush, like the gasping call of a runner preceding a procession.

Then, when the water swelled so slightly, he glimpsed her turning in the flashing white light, like a mayfly nymph struggling from its filmy slip. Did she beckon him? In an instant, she disappeared. He did not see her again that night, though he remained staring into the spring and listening through the night.

Through the following days his old patterns began breaking down. He returned at all hours to sit by the spring, his senses open to its sounds and glancing rhythms as never before. Even when the moon faded again he spent his nights there, wakeful and expectant, as if his whole life depended on seeing her fully or hearing what she might speak to him.

At first he saw her rarely, turning in the water or lifting partly from its film. Then one day, just at dawn, he saw her emerge, lifting her gleaming body from the pure water. She hung momentarily before his dazed eyes, her damp translucent wings fanning the bright air. She disappeared into the cool shadows.

From that dawning the hermit saw her almost every day, but so fleetingly or at such a distance that he distrusted his eyes. Now he reasoned with himself: Perhaps she was the creation of his old dry longing; perhaps he was mistaking the ephemeral life of spring for something holy; perhaps his long solitude and dreaming had made him mad.

But he believed that she was real and holy, something linked to the meaning of his life. He began to call to her, to make songs for her. His voice was brittle and unsure from so much silence. From years of unspoken thought, from a lifetime in which his musings and the processes of nature were interchanged, he had lost the ability to tell when he began speaking and when he stopped, when he was feeling the world around him and when he was merely reflecting on it. The roots stirred in his dreams and the new birds sang his joy and whirled after each other in his fringed thoughts, confusing him.

Thus. when he saw her arise again from the dancing water and drift off slowly among the trees, he followed after her, calling to her with a voice that got lost among the incantations of the spring. And he knew she would not wait for him, perhaps was not even real, as he hurried away from his clearing into dark places where he had never been and from which he knew he would never return.

The Songbird

Within a walled yard, gray and bare, a small bent man carried stones from one side to the other. He moved with mechanical regularity and great energy, as if he was caught in the discipline of some important work. He set the stones carefully, side by side and mounting upward, as if to put them in readiness for some still larger undertaking.

But nothing was being built in this small closed place. If you had watched him a long time, you would have seen that he was locked in an endless circle: that, once all the stones were set on one side of the yard, he would start back again. With hardly a break, he would begin to reset them on the opposite side. The stones were like beads on a rosary that one works through his fingers, back and forth, long after he has stopped praying.

A bare fruit tree stood in the middle of the yard, desolate in the gray March air. One day, a brilliant bird settled in its branches. Song flowed out of it as from a fountain and its music filled the yard like the fragrance of new blossoms. The man stopped and put down his heavy stone, letting the bird song bathe him. Lifting his bowed face, he stared at the glittering bird—-and hated his life.

Looking down again, he found a sharp cold stone at his feet. The stone fit hard and dead in his hand. In one motion, unthinking and yet sure (as if he had practiced this many times before) he flung the stone through the branches close where the joyful bird was poised, careful not to hit her but near enough to chase her away, forever.

The Labyrinth

The carriage rocked gently along a dusty road. It was already mid-morning. The warmth of the sun and the peace of the countryside lulled the carriage's only passenger into drowsiness. He was a gentleman in middle age, portly and comfortable with himself. This business journey had required him to arise earlier than usual, and he dozed now to be fresh when he arrived. It would be a long ride back to his family when he returned that evening.

He felt the carriage stop. Looking out, he saw the driver unhitch the horses and lead them to a stream: they needed water and rest. The gentleman decided to stretch his legs by strolling a bit in the woods that adjoined the road. A narrow path led off among the trees, inviting him.

As soon as he entered the cool green world under the trees he was renewed. The moving green floor of the woods was speckled with yellow light, and the air was alive. Birds appeared and disappeared, magically, and large bright butterflies floated silently around him. Then he heard the soft melodious call of a thrush, alluring and remote.

Looking down the winding path he saw a child seated on a log, a young girl, pensive and clothed in white. He thought she might be lost: surely, she was very sad. He started to call out, but did not, for fear he would frighten her. Then, she arose and turned down the path deeper into the woods.

He knew the driver would be waiting, but he had to see the girl again. Perhaps she needed his help. Now he was hurrying after her. Several times he thought he heard singing ahead, but when he stopped to listen he only heard bird song and his own difficult breathing. He was ready to turn back when he saw her in a small clearing. She wasn't a child, nor was she crying. She was chasing butterflies and laughing, her motions lithe as a dancer's. She paused and looked back at him, her green eyes sparkling. Suddenly he wanted to run and dance too. He found himself weaving back and forth across the clearing, scarcely aware how he was puffing as they followed the meandering flight of the butterflies. They were laughing together and their hands stretched upward, mimicking the butterflies.

When she finally stopped, he was panting and had to sink to the ground to catch his breath. She leaned calmly against a large dark tree and turned to him. Now he saw clearly that she was a woman, and her beauty broke into his chambered heart. She smiled quietly and turned away, moving toward the path once more. The gentleman hurried to his feet, unaware of how sweaty and disheveled his fine business clothes had become.

His pace quickened as she disappeared before him. The trail was narrow, with bushes leaning in on both sides, their barbs catching at him continually. It twisted and doubled back, so that several times he was sure he was crossing his own path. One moment he would lose sight of her running before him, the next he would come quite close. She looked back over her shoulder and he saw that her eyes were dark now, and still. Was it enticement or terror that he saw there? He was unsure whether she ran from him to ensnare him or to escape him. Nor did he know why he continued to struggle after her.

When he could continue no longer, he stopped by a large damp boulder. Although the sun was directly overhead, it barely pierced the heavy dome of branches. This place was open, with low green ferns and a surprising coolness. He wanted to lie down and rest. His clothes were tattered and his breath came with great difficulty. He thought to look where the path might lead away from this opening, but could find no exit. Then he realized that there was a small dark cave in the clearing and it breathed cool air out to him. Approaching it, he saw her just inside. She seemed tired and old, but unafraid now. Slowly he went in to her without a thought of the carriage which stood waiting for him on the bright straight road.

The Whirlpool

A village maiden was hurrying along a trail when she met a nymph sunning herself at the edge of a mountain stream. Although she had never seen such a creature before, it seemed right to greet her. Looking at the cold white form, she felt happy in her warm fleshy beauty. It suddenly seemed supremely good to be a mortal peasant girl. When she told the nymph she was going to meet her beloved, the nymph smiled icily. She asked whether the girl was sure of her beloved. Perhaps even a cold ethereal spirit could turn his heart away from her. The girl accepted the challenge without a thought.

This was the match. The nymph would have some moments to entrance the young man before the maiden came to him. Then he would say which of them was loveliest. The maid felt triumphant already as she watched the nymph depart. The nymph could use no magic wiles, for nymphs cannot lie. And since they have no heart, there was only sport to guide her art. But the maiden had all her warm cunning and her fleshy bond with the lad. She smiled complacently in anticipation as she waited the brief moments.

The mountain stream surged out of the foothills into the broad deep river, making a strong slow whirlpool. There her peasant lad sat on the bank watching the icy green water coil into the silted brown water of the river. He tossed sticks down and watched them get captured in long easy circles, letting his thoughts follow them dreamily.

At first they circled so widely that they seemed caught in the general flow of the river. But then the circles began to narrow, tightening down steadily, closing to quick short spins, and disappearing, soundlessly.

He had almost forgotten he was awaiting his beloved. Each afternoon they met there when their day's work was done. She was his first love and would be his wife. His boyhood had flowed into youth so easily, following the steady ways of his village. And now manhood was upon him and he would continue into that without a break. These afternoons were like the few days during which the apple trees flare up in blossoms before the long quiet green of summer. Bees buzzed busily around him and he was dimly aware that his love was late.

The nymph appeared to the youth from the stream's mouth. She came wet and gleaming up to him, flashing under the afternoon sun. "Do not be startled fair lad. I have just come to look at your beauty and warm myself by it as by a gentle flame. Do not be afraid: I have no love to give you." The youth was caught up in awe by her radiance. Her voice was like pure white light, hiding nothing and shining right into him. Her eyes were greener than the mountain stream and they drew him in. For a moment he wondered if his beloved would come and find them like this. But he was already in the nymph's hold. He stood up and went toward her. But the nymph withdrew to the river's edge. "You cannot touch me, gentle youth, though you are handsome and good. I must go now. Look well, for you shall not see me again." With these words she sank away.

Just then the maiden came, finding her love gazing down into the river. She stood proudly above him, glowing with the sun's warmth. "Come up to me you silly boy. She was just a heartless nymph, cold as a fish. Here, take my hand. Look away now. She could not love you. I know that she will never come back; she told me so herself. Come take me in your arms my sweet boy and let's walk in the fields the way we always do."

But even then his feet were at the water's edge. He stepped out into the river with mindless certainty. Then the water lifted him, catching him in the long slow sweep of the whirlpool. The maiden watched in mute disbelief as the river took her love, drawing him in steadily until he was spinning like a little boat. Then he disappeared, soundlessly.

The Willow Crib

She was three months big with his love-child when he left. That afternoon she had begun to weave a crib from the pliant willows along the river. As they sat close by the fire in the chilly evening, words and thoughts mingling with the flames and sounds as they always did, he questioned her about what she was making. She felt his voice turn hard as she told him of the glory that she bore and of her joy. That night he seemed far away, though he enfolded her as always. He told her again of his difficult life and why he had to return. She thought she felt him shudder as they made love in the big darkness of the house. Then, when he kissed her goodnight, his large hand caressed her swelling lower body and he said, "Put it away when it comes, my love. Do that for me." She did not understand, but she said "Yes." And all was well as she drifted into sleep, peaceful as a child beside its mother.

When she awoke, he was gone. At first she was bewildered, searching over the farm for him. Then she felt a painful anger that he could leave her at this time. In the following days she settled into a long sadness and the comforting routines of her simple life. Each day the child grew in her soft body, renewing her love of the world and her life and her lover.

She had come up to this remote country just at the beginning of spring. Her blind aunt had sent a message that the farmhands were leaving when the planting was finished. She had come up to the farm to help. He had arrived just after the planting began, taking a room at the back of the cottage. The doctors had prescribed a long rest in the country, for the fresh air and the slow peaceful life.

Their union was inevitable. She was like the meadows for him, open and innocent; her laughter like flowers in a field of hay. He was a remote holy splendor for her, and his love a ceaseless adoration. Their love grew seamlessly, from working together in the fields to sitting quietly at table to embracing as the hills curve to the sky. It was all one circle of new life together.

Then the fall came on. The crib was finished and set to dry by the fireplace. She was alone with her invalid aunt, who remained almost invisible in her inner room. There were no meddling eyes to see her grow big with the burden of his love. As winter set in, she sat by the fire each evening, stroking her round belly and dreaming in her simplicity of the boy she would bear. Her young breasts swelled and she dreamed of suckling him, letting him grow from her body as he grew away into manhood. One day he would find his beloved and leave his mother: she knew it was silly to think so far ahead, but it hurt her nonetheless.

It was in the depth of winter, at the very turning of the year, when her time came. She was alone, except for the sightless old woman she cared for. She delivered herself alone. All through the night she held the infant close. Toward morning she awakened, feeling the small mouth moving against her. How she ached to take him to her breast, to let his delicate mouth find her sweet pap and live. Her strong hands shook as she held him away. "My sweet dear, who grew out of my very soul, my innocent love, I cannot keep you. So long ago I promised to put you away. I did not dream how beautiful you would be and how I would long to hold you to my heart. Forgive me what I must do.

The floor was cold as she searched by the darkened fireplace for the willow crib. Wrapping the babe in a light cover, she placed him in the crib and carried him to the river bank. The eastern sky was just opening as she knelt by the frozen shore. Her mind was all confusion as she set the frail vessel on the moving water. "Farewell dear love, my baby Jesus; sail on my little Moses." She had been alone so long with her burden of love that she barely understood what she was doing as she gave the child to the river.

Two Birds

A village maiden lived with her widowed mother in a quiet hidden life. She was a seamstress who helped support their simple life by sewing, making traditional dresses for women in the village and occasional festive garments for weddings and such. Though naturally cheerful and outgoing, she was sometimes pensive in her silent life, recalling stories her grandmother had told her as a child. She loved to read in the small collection of books of poetry and romance her grandmother had left behind after her passing. Sometimes she played softly on the simple flute she also inherited, traditional dancing songs and haunting ballad refrains.

One day she was sitting in their tiny walled garden, wistfully playing fragments of old melodies that drifted through her dreaming head, letting vague yearnings rise and disappear. It seemed like some of the wild birds were drawn to her music, even joining in her songs as they flitted about in a flowering fruit tree. Then the maiden heard a pure strong birdsong flowing from the throat of a small golden warbler. She sat entranced as the music swelled and spilled over the garden in a near ecstasy of song. It lifted the girl's spirits more than anything had ever done, and she knew she had to find a way to keep that bird close to her.

She remembered a tale from her grandmother about how to capture your heart's desire, and immediately a way appeared to her. There was an old woven willow birdcage still stored in their attic from her grandmother's belongings. Afraid the bird would fly away before she could return, the maiden scrambled in the attic and hurried back. Setting the cage on the ground, the maiden sprinkled a trail of bread crumbs leading into the open cage door. Wonderfully, the golden bird was still hopping among the blossoms, chirping quietly as it searched for something. When the girl took up her flute and began playing a gentle romantic melody the bird paused to listen. Spontaneously, the bird began to warble and sing as if in response to the maiden's flute, and she felt an instant identity with the bird. Gradually it moved closer until it spied the crumbs. Flitting to the ground, it started pecking at the bread, its tiny beak cautiously trying each crumb before taking it. Soon it was so caught up in feeding that it unwittingly entered the cage. The maiden quickly shut the door and her heart beat with joy and excitement.

When she carried the cage into the house the maiden worried that she was terrifying the warbler, but it soon grew calm. When evening came the girl covered the cage with a cloth, watching the tiny golden creature close its eyes and drift into a deep sleep. In the morning the girl was awakened by unfamiliar sounds coming from her bedside. The warbler was stirring, fluttering its delicate wings and making soft purring sounds in its throat. From that day on the girl's spirits lifted as the bird became more playful and sang and hopped about with joy. Making sure the house was closed, she opened the cage door and encouraged the bird to come out. Tentatively, it came close to the opening and peeked out. Then it hopped onto a nearby table and began lifting its voice. Soon that was part of their daily pattern: the little bird waking the girl, being let out into the small room, and then flying about as the girl laid out their breakfast.

One day the maiden was talking to her "sweet bird" and "little friend" when she had an inspiration: she should name the bird Layla after the beautiful girl in an old sad love story her grandmother had once told her. It did seem like the bird was lonely and filled with longing, even when it perched on the furniture and flooded the room with song. When the maiden saw Layla sitting on the window sill gazing out, it seemed like the bird was remembering its life of freedom in the wild. What if it had been separated from its life mate? Perhaps it was selfish to have captured this lovely free spirit and kept it in this small closed world. The maiden's doubts only deepened when Layla began to grow quiet and subdued, rarely leaving her cage.

Then one day a wandering merchant came to the village, his two-wheeled cart drawn by a tired old horse and piled high with a miscellany of goods. The girl recalled him, or someone like him, passing through the village in years past. Toward evening she and her mother followed other villagers to the shaded grove where the merchant was camped. He had arrayed all his goods for people to see and examine. On blankets spread on the grass were tin ware, gleaming knives, necklaces and ear rings, stacks of antique fabrics and garments, small rare books, exotic musical instruments, and many other curiosities. From the cart hung small lanterns, ceramic jugs, beautiful old rugs, and many other things that seemed to be from another world.

Browsing with her mother, the maiden was carefully examining small bundles of rich fabrics and picking through wooden boxes filled with ornamental beads and buttons. When she looked up, the merchant was leaning over them awaiting their questions. He was a short dark mysterious man, with black eyes and even blacker hair drawn back in a ponytail. The maiden saw that he was one of those ageless creatures, one moment an ancient wise man and the next an enthusiastic laughing boy.

The merchant was discussing the price of some small items with the maiden's mother when some boys began rummaging in the cart. They wondered what the many-stringed instrument was and what music could be played upon it. Excusing himself, the merchant indulged the boys by bringing out the lute and showing it to the boys. Then he was tuning the strings and gently strumming them until all were in tune. Suddenly he began plucking the strings almost magically as an elegant light dancing song leaped from the lute. Everyone fell silent as the music danced around the cart. Then an exquisite voice joined the music, like some tiny flute moving in perfect harmony with the strings. It was the voice of a bird coming from the depths of the covered cart.

When the song was finished there was a hush. The maiden was struck by the bird's clear delicate song, so like her Layla. She thanked the merchant and asked about the beautiful birdsong. He offered to show her and then was climbing into the cart to bring out a wire cage. In it was perched a golden warbler, the very image of Layla. As she started to explain her amazement, telling the story of her Layla, the merchant clapped his hand to his forehead and shook himself in disbelief. "My dear bird is Majnun," he said. "He came to me two years ago when I was encamped beside a mountain stream. Sometimes he is wild and crazy, but his heart is pure and he sings like an angel." As they talked some more the merchant explained that Majnun had been growing quiet and withdrawn and he worried about the bird's health. When they parted, the maiden invited the merchant to her small home so he could see Layla for himself.

The very next morning the merchant appeared at their doorstep, his cart packed and ready to continue their journey. As he dismounted the cart he brought the cage with him, carrying it into the house. Layla was still in her cage, softly murmuring as she picked at her seeds. In response, Majnun started chirping and warbling. The sounds immediately transfixed Layla and she started to respond in her own melodious ways. The merchant was thrilled by the sudden rejuvenation of his dear friend. He said this was destiny, that the two birds just had to be together as if they had been seeking each other for so long. In a little while the merchant said he needed to set forth on the road. It seemed to the maiden that he was hurrying so he would not have a change of heart and take Majnun with him. The maiden embraced the mysterious man and wished him safe journey, promising that she would always care for the two birds.

In subsequent weeks and months, the house was filled with a new jubilation. Now the maiden was roused from her dreams by the chattering of two golden birds. When she opened their shared cage, they flew out and swirled around the room, chasing and playing with each other. It made the maiden's heart ache with happiness to see the young lovers so utterly absorbed in each other. When Majnun began carrying threads and feathers and other small soft things into the cage the girl realized he was creating a nest. Were they preparing to have a family?

But then, as Layla began to refine the nest, Majnun seemed to withdraw, to sulk in a corner and refuse to leave the cage. It seemed that Layla was trying to distract him, to entice him from his melancholy. But nothing helped. One morning the maiden opened a window to let the fresh summer breeze cleanse the room. When she began to prepare breakfast, she suddenly realized that Majnun had disappeared. He had escaped through the window. Dashing outside she looked all over the walled yard with no success. She called his name but got no response. Back inside, she wept close to the cage with Layla perching close beside her. She felt that she had foolishly betrayed her joyous bird.

All that day and for many after the maiden searched for Majnun. When Layla was safely in her cage she would open the window hoping for Majnun's return. But it was in vain. Gradually, Layla also began to withdraw and grow silent, sometimes immobilized all day in her cage. The maiden couldn't bear to remove the abandoned nest. Now when the little bird perched on the window sill it was clear that she longed to follow after Majnun. Layla had become the maiden's dearest companion, but now the girl realized that she had to release the golden singer back into the world.

So, one afternoon, she carried the cage into the walled yard and said her last goodbyes. "Dear Layla, you are my very heart, so I must know your longing for Majnun. I so much need to keep you for my comfort and my consolation. But too well I feel the yearning that calls you out into the world to find your beloved." The girl was sobbing as her trembling hand drew back the latch to open the cage door. Layla sat still for a moment, looking intently at the maiden. Then, in a flurry, she flew out, circled the fruited tree, and perched high on its crown. There she released a fountain of song, at once plaintive and joyous. Soaring over the garden wall came a small golden warbler, singing in midflight. It was Majnun, and when he alighted beside Layla, his lady, the maiden's heart soared up with them.

The Wind

He stood upon a high hill. This vantage was for the monarch only. From it he could view his island realm in perfect summary, and all was well. The fields were freshly tilled, ready for planting. Orchards were coming into bloom. Vineyards drowsed on sunny hillsides in pale new green. He could see two villages, washed white by spring rains. Here and there a farmer was at work or on the road, and tiny people moved upon the village streets. It was all silent and remote, like a puppet show in miniature. His gaze wandered contentedly over this world, with no impulse to think of the island beyond his sight, for it was all as this; with no need to consider an uncertain future, since this year would repeat a familiar cycle; and with no inclination to think of any world beyond this realm, for it was all unknown. A burst of warm air ruffled his gray hair. He turned to the west, where the afternoon sea gleamed so brightly he could not look to the horizon.

He was a monarch without a queen. But although he was already in midlife, there was no need of that, nor any possibility. Wasn't his domain secure without alliances, and rich without trade beyond its shores? Weren't his subjects his children, and didn't his counsel and command beget all that they required? Anyway, it would not do to take a peasant girl to wife, and contact with other worlds was lost in his father's youth. And there were court players to amuse and delight him.

Toward evening he wandered in the gardens encircling his palace, his thoughts like the golden fish floating in the ponds. The air was still. Ornamental trees breathed their refined fragrances, making pools of sweet air in which he drifted. He came close to the great stone wall that needlessly separated the gardens from the virgin forests beyond it. A cool stream of pungent air washed over him from the dark trees. The monarch shivered and thrilled vaguely at the scent — spices.

Like a school boy, he pulled himself to the top of the wall and peered over it. Two deer browsed in the small clearing that lay between the wall and the primeval forest. A narrow glittering stream wandered out of the great trees, winding across the grassy meadow, and passing under a low arch in the wall. So that was where the courtyard stream came from. Dusk was near, and night was already waiting under the dense boughs of the forest. The monarch felt the cool air breath toward him, and the fragrances touched him again. Climbing down, he walked slowly toward the trees, where no ax had ever struck.

It was then that he first saw her. A young woman seated on a large mossy rock close to the stream where it appeared from the forest. She was luminous, with long golden hair and a white gown. The gown was of simple design, loose and flowing like the peasant women wore, but it had an unearthly quality. Perhaps it was the way the soft breeze played in it and her moving hair. The fragrance seemed to flow from her.

The maiden appeared to be lost in gazing into the stream. Suddenly, the monarch realized he was spying and might startle her. Without thinking why, he shrugged off his royal cape and removed the splendid medallion that hung at his breast. Striding across the meadow, he could have been a peasant himself in his casual shirt and hiking trousers. When the deer bolted, she turned toward him in perfect calm. He was struck through by her unfamiliar beauty, stopping in full stride. No words came, not even a thought of words. He simply raised a hand in greeting. By some gesture, so slight he later could not describe it, perhaps a mere widening of her eyes, she welcomed him.

When they began to speak, their words were few and simple: about the beauty of this place, the emerging dusk, the serenity. Somehow, he said he lived close by and asked whether she had a place to stay the evening. He did not inquire how she came to be here or where her home was. She did not question his identity. There was a mystery of presence, resting wholly in an enchanted moment.

Slowly, they walked toward the wall. He made a foothold with his linked hands and she deftly reached the top, lowering a hand to help him up. She showed no surprise at the gardens and courtyard nor even at the palace within. The monarch made provisions for her dinner and lodging and bade her goodnight.

The story of the following days, indeed, well into the summer, is long to tell. But, in short, that spring and summer passed like endless play. Surely the monarch assumed this woman would one day be his queen; but he never sought out her origins or distant wishes. Even while dreaming that she would be with him forever, he took her for a passing grace.

Each day they rose early, before breezes came to dry the dew. He would send servants to her chamber and she would come to some new secret place (a balcony, patio or alcove) that he had chosen. The palace seemed as it had been in his boyhood—intricate, ancient and magical. Then they would dine lightly on peasant bread, fruit and spring water, wondering together where the winds of fancy would take them this day. Soon they were off to the forest, the windblown hills or the empty beaches.

In the dark forest she would often run before him, disappearing among great ferns and the massive vaulted trees, startling deer from their browse and sending grouse in a flurry from their cover. These signs and her shouts of delight would bring the monarch to her again: perhaps beside a spring bubbling out of mossy rocks or sprawling in a clearing bright with summer flowers. Then she would let him catch her. And when he held her, these things were rare indeed.

Always, some servants struggled after them, bearing baskets of food, parasols, towels, a kite, or whatever the spirit of the day suggested. At times the servants hurried desperately so as not to lose track of the romping couple; at times they dozed discreetly out of sight while the couple lingered. They even carried the monarch's daybook, in which he could review figures on production, plans for construction and other enterprises. But now his mind was far from business, and when he called for the daybook, it was to set down some image or song or other flow of words.

"How like a leaf upon the waters my lady moves among the flowers."

"The wind plays in the fountain's plume: your laughter moves through me so."

"This fair afternoon: everything alive and bright with motion, yet time has disappeared."

"There is the infinite beyond (the star-sprinkled heavens, the dark well of the past) and there is the infinite within (this drying seed pod, this very moment."

Such things startled him at times, like unfamiliar birds roosting in the orchard. But he was drawn to musings and playful trifles. It did not occur to him to share these with his lady as he lounged jotting in his book, lazily attending to her wonderfully free activities.

One day they were dining in the very heart of the forest, reclining beside a little stream that came whispering out of a cool grove and disappeared wordlessly from the small clearing. The servants had set up a silk tent, and when their meal was done the maiden went into it to rest in the hushed afternoon. Sitting a little way off, the monarch meditated on the tent. What a slight thing could separate them or conceal his beloved from him. Then it seemed the brilliant tent breathed like a great butterfly under the invisible touch of the gentle wind. He would have called for his daybook, but he had drifted into a dream: she was transformed into a glowing butterfly, fluttering before his futile reach.

Another day they were ranging over some grassy hills along the sea. The wind swept over them, making the tall grass wave and hiss like the green seas surging far below. The monarch rested beneath a large parasol that the servants had managed to secure against the wind. He was watching his beloved sailing a rainbow-hued kite in the gusting air. At first, she ran before the lifting wing; then it rose higher and higher, and she let the delicate line flow upward into the shimmering sky. Now the kite floated serenely, as if transcending the gusting winds below. It seemed to the monarch that the kite was suspended among the rounded clouds beside it: they were like ponderous whales floating on the surface of some distant sea. He and his lady were beneath a vast blue sea, and the sunlight slanted down to them in their soundless world. The kite bobbed like some fisherman's float, and the line sloped down to her.

From the beginning, the monarch's counsellors were troubled by his new ways and his absorption in the play of a mere girl. He could not help seeing them cluster like chickens muttering among themselves. Guardedly, they spoke within his hearing about royal traditions, propriety and caution. Their talk was abstract, but pointed. Then there were vocal questions about the lady's origins and lineage. Shouldn't there be plans for a wedding? The people of the island should know of these things. The monarch heard all of this and assented in his mind, but he did not speak of them with her.

With her it was a continual dalliance and delight. Even in the night, with each still sleeping in separate chambers, his thoughts went out to her endlessly. One sultry evening he walked in the courtyard outside her chamber, listening to her talking with her handmaiden as the bath was prepared. The splashing water drowned the sense of their words, but it was the sound of children innocently together. He ached for her. Soon it was still, except for the warm night air washing through the windows and caressing his beloved as she rose from her bath and slowly dried herself. He wanted to possess her, now and always. The next day he secretly called two older ladies of the court for their counsel and set them to laying plans for a wedding.

One day they were picnicking and sailing by the edge of the sea. She sat in the bow of the frail craft and let him tend the tiller as they glided up and down the shoreline. They went ashore to build fantastic things in the sand. After lunch the girl returned to the boat, cruising alone along the sea's edge. The monarch leaned idly under a parasol, watching his beloved gliding back and forth under the gleaming sail. The wind suddenly dropped away, becalming the little boat. Then, turning on some silent center, the wind began to blow seaward, growing with each gust. The boat turned like a fish, the bright sail puffed full, and it pushed away from land. The monarch realized that his lady was being swept away. He called desperately to her, but she did not seem to hear. He could not see if she was trying to turn back or even if she looked back to him. Helplessly, he watched the boat become small as a toy, and then it disappeared.

The monarch remained at the water's edge until darkness covered everything. Perhaps the wind would turn again, or she would learn how to work back against the strong wind. There was no violent weather, and winter was far off. Tomorrow would bring calm and sunlit skies. The servants waited mute; in the darkness they led their grieving master home, like tragic friends.

The next day and through the following weeks the monarch compelled his bravest men to take to the sea in their small fishing boats. But they were not sailors, and the sea was vast. Even a remnant of the sail or the little boat broken on some shore would have been a comfort. But the winds and tides did not give as much as that.

The monarch sank from hopeful anxiety to disbelief, from disbelief to despair, from despair to immobilizing grief. Then a great rage began to arise in him, and he swore he would subdue the winds that had taken his beloved. He called the chief sorcerers to his court and commanded them to silence the wind forever. His counsellors tried to reason with him: his kingdom needed wind to bring the rains, to cool summer days, to turn the mill wheels. And it is futile and perhaps dangerous to meddle with such things. But he would hear none of this.

The sorcerers labored day and night, searching their most obscure books and invoking every dark power they knew, but all was in vain. In his rage, the monarch ordered the execution of the chief sorcerer. Days of calm came, but only to taunt him. One day he walked in the village and heard the flapping of clothing hung in backyards to dry. He ordered that all laundry be taken down whenever the wind blew. The sound of leaves rustling pained him and the lapping of waves was unbearable. At last, he yielded to those who said that no skill or power of man could close up the wind. There was no hope of that.

Then he had a wonderful idea: he could close himself from any wind. He determined never again to leave his palace, except at times of perfect calm. On blustery days every window was sealed, and the monarch remained deep within the palace. But still it was insufficient.

So, he called together his best architects to design a castle of perfect stillness, where not the faintest movement of air could enter or arise.

Through the following year his mind was only on the plans for and then the construction of his castle. It would be surrounded by high walls to break any wind before it could reach the castle. A great entry chamber provided a series of boxes within boxes which one had to pass through in sequence, from the carriage entrance to the inmost door, each door beyond remaining sealed until the door behind was closed. The castle walls were bare, since any tapestries would stir from the mere motions of people. Every candle was enclosed in a globe so not even the least breath of air would make a flame flicker needlessly. If it had been possible, only sun and moon would have lit the inmost places.

New regulations occurred to the monarch almost daily. Servants and people of the court were to enter only for necessities: their clothing had to be close-fitting so as not to stir up motions, and their feet clad in soft slippers; there could be no sudden gestures or rapid movements; all speaking must be soft and quiet and never directly toward the monarch.

Finally, the castle was completed. When a day of perfect calm came, the monarch rode in his sealed carriage to the castle. It passed through the high gates and entered the first chamber, where one could disembark beyond any touch of natural winds. As he moved through the series of entrance rooms the monarch was delighted with how his plans had been realized. At last he reached the inmost place, his private chambers, where he could dwell alone, never to be touched or fretted by any wind again.

The Potion

There was a lady, well favored in beauty and happy disposition. She was married to a nobleman and her life was circled about by three lovely children and finery and large gardens. Her days were filled with joy and her nights with ease and gentle sleep.

It happened that a young man fell in love with her. As if in a story, he was a wandering musician, given to dreaming over his lute and his old fanciful songs. When first he saw this lady his heart lept and her beauty cut through him with the most exquisite pain. He was struck silent, made mute with longing.

He learned almost at once that she was a married woman of position, with three dear children. For days he drifted around the village, torn by his love of her. He played with children in the streets and walked among the tombstones. One moment he whistled and laughed; the next he sighed and hummed forgotten dirges.

One day he sat by the wall outside her gardens. He watched the butterflies dancing among the flowers, and their joy was his joy. He saw a fat gray slug crawling in the cool shade of a rock, and felt it was he. He took up his lute and began to pluck out an antique love song, very fragile and full of little agonies. His voice joined the instrument's plaintive voice, high and delicate, and his soul was all open in the simple ancient words.

The lady had come down to the garden to be alone among her flowers in the dreamy afternoon. She heard the lute begin, and it seemed to her that the butterflies rose and fell, drifted and fluttered down, in time with it. Her heart was touched, and when she heard the young man's voice carrying the beautiful old song it flowed into her.

She was close by the wall, and looking over it she saw the young man seated on a stone. Her gaze enclosed him just as he felt her presence and looked up to her. He was all dazzled and dumb inside, but he found his voice enough to say, "Good day my lady. What a fine bright garden you have." And she knew that he loved her, and was hurt for that. She said, "Thank you, gentle sir. But no garden is lovely enough to call forth so rare a song. Play on please, but something with no clouds or shadows for this sweet afternoon." And he knew she loved him, for his love and for his hurt. He put off all sorrow and played a quick bright dancing song for her, wanting her to forget his sadness. She laughed and her eyes flashed and she waved cheerfully to him as he went down the lane. But a sliver of pain touched her heart, and he felt the selfsame pain.

Each day, then, he passed her garden trying to sing light easy songs to conceal his suffering: but she heard his sadness through the playful words. He thought of simply leaving as he had come. Then she would hear him no more and never be reminded of his sad love for her. But he knew she would understand his departure and her heart would follow after him and remember him and stay burdened with compassion for him.

It was then that he recalled a potion described in an old song. Unlike that familiar drink or spell which lovers use to capture their beloved, this was a potion to dry up the most vigorous longing. For he did love this lady so dearly that he would undo his very love for the sake of her happiness. As he gathered the herbs and juices, and spoke the incantations, he thought how easy it is to die for love or to be separated forever from one's beloved. What could be sweeter than such death, and what more delicious agony than a life of wandering apart from a changeless pure beloved?

Then the potion was prepared, and he lifted it to his young lips. "Tomorrow, if you chance to see me, my dear lady, my only love, you will mark a great change in me. You will see me indifferent to you, perhaps following the skirts of some village girl. And then you can think how fickle a young man's heart can be, and how foolish a lady's. And you will laugh and wave to me, free of this hopeless burden. And, perchance, I will see you and wave back, without understanding anything." He let her image stand beautiful and still before his mind one last time, and then he drank the potion down, deeply and surely.

The Guardian Angel

The jeweler's apprentice was a peasant lad who came to the city to learn a trade. One day the king and queen rode through the streets of the city, returning to their castle in a royal procession. The apprentice stood at the shop window gazing in awe at the splendor of the mounted guards, the musicians and the regal carriage. The king and queen glittered in the sunlight, waving to the people in the streets. It was then that he first saw the princess. She sat in a corner of the carriage upon a velvet seat, serene and radiant. Her beauty exceeded that of the rarest gem and burned into the young man's heart.

Throughout the following year, her image flamed in the crucible of his dreams, though he did not see her again. When he had a day of rest he would hike into the countryside toward the castle, hoping to see her. But he never did. From time to time he overheard women gossiping about the royal family and his ears were open for every word about the princess. He learned that she played upon the harp exquisitely, that she sang like a rare bird, and that no maiden of the court danced so lightly and freely as she. She cared for orphaned children and took compassion on the servants, often interceding on their behalf. Each word he heard confirmed his dreams and deepened his hopeless longing.

Then word went out that the princess was promised in marriage. A noble prince was to come from a far-off land to take her for his wife. The day came when he was to arrive in the city to parade through the streets with the princess to celebrate their betrothal. The apprentice was torn asunder, rejoicing that he would see her once more and grieving that she was to marry and travel to a remote land. When the procession passed the jeweler's shop he watched, hidden inside. The prince was handsome, with regal bearing. But the apprentice imagined that the princess concealed some sadness as she waved and smiled to the people who cheered along the way.

The very next day the prince came into the jeweler's shop, seeking a special wedding gift made by local craftsmen. The old jeweler excitedly showed him all of his largest and rarest gems, set in the most elegant ways. Then the prince noticed some delicate figures cast in pure gold—-cupids and angels and dancing forms of an almost magical vitality. The jeweler told him they were the work of his most gifted apprentice. Perhaps the prince would wish something designed especially for his bride. The apprentice was called to the front of the shop. When he saw the prince and heard his desires his mind soared.

He spoke with passion to the prince. Jewels should not be considered. Cold and hard, they glittered faceted and lifeless in any setting. Gold, gold is the thing. Gold shaped into some touching figure suited to embody the warmth of perfect love. Did the prince know where gold comes from? There is no alchemist's magic to transform base metal into yellow gold. Gold is formed deep in the earth, under the mountains, where few men dare venture. He told of how the earth longs for the sky and how, in the deepest night, they embrace, the earth opening to the infinite night and the sky embracing her utterly. This it is that yields up gold in the body of the earth, the residue of longing and deep passion. That is why gold, though it is indissoluble by the most corrosive acids, glows with light and warmth.

The prince saw that the young man was inspired. When the apprentice suggested that he design a guardian angel cast in the finest gold, the prince thought it would make the perfect gift. The figure was to be a pendant for a delicate necklace. It had to be ready for the wedding day, just two days ahead.

As soon as the prince left the shop the apprentice set to work. The jeweler gladly provided his most precious gold, a small pouch of nuggets flecked with a rare pink and brought from an unknown land. The apprentice worked into the night without rest, carving the minute wax model with all the care of his exception skill and his passion for the princess. The tiny angel emerged from the hard wax like a living being, its fragile wings opened and its tiny arms extended in benediction. Then the plaster mold was formed around the model and set to dry. The apprentice slept in the shop until dawn: the angel kept rising from the darkness of his dreams, seeking the princess and hovering over her. When the other workers returned the following day he was already firing the gold, tending it constantly to remove even the slightest impurities. As the second night came on he was in the shop alone again. Now the mold was ready to receive the pure molten gold. His hand trembled as he poured the glowing liquid, and he heard the wax evaporate at its intense touch.

When the jeweler arrived early the next morning, he found the mold on the apprentice's workbench, cooled but still closed. He thought that the apprentice should break it open and finish the figure, but the wedding day was at hand and the prince's servant would soon come for the pendant. Taking up his small hammer, he tapped the plaster mold and it broke away cleanly from the figure.

The figure was so small and light that it fell to the wooden bench quietly as a feather. The jeweler could not believe his eyes: the angel was barely an inch high, but it glowed with a golden life that made it seem capable of flight. He had thought to finish it with his tools, but the apprentice had cast the mold so precisely that there was not the slightest rough edge or imperfection in the figure. The jeweler found his finest chain and suspended the angel from it. When the servant came, he paid handsomely for the necklace. The jeweler meant to give a generous part of the payment to his apprentice, but he never saw him again.

That afternoon, when the wedding ceremony was over and the royal couple stood in the midst of their guests opening their luxurious gifts, the prince embraced his bride and gave her a small box. The princess knew it was his finest gift, and her eyes scarcely left her new husband as she opened the lid. She was touched as never before at the sight of the tiny figure lying on its velvet couch. She took off her jeweled necklace and encircled her fine white neck with the simple chain, letting the winged figure rest on her pure breast.

The banquet and the royal ball followed, but in the midst of all the festivity she felt a flame of love flare up in her breast at the touch of the angel. It was as if an infinity of love was magically compressed in the small figure, making a charm to shield and comfort her forever.

The Lure of the Beloved
Three Stories

I - The Blind Woodcarver

As was his habit, the middle-aged woodcarver was indulging in a short nap after his midday meal. The daybed was close to an open window, which looked out onto the fenced yard. A soft spring breeze stirred the curtains and filled the small cabin with the scents and gentle sounds of wakening life.

In the middle world between waking and sleeping, he was carried along in a stream of images. It seemed he was still a boy watching his mother as she bent over the woodstove stirring a pot of stew, absorbed in her familiar work as she hummed some old melody to herself. The sunlight streamed in and made a pale golden halo around her head, illuminating her silver hair. He wanted to say something to her, but hesitated to break the domestic spell which encircled her. Then she disappeared at what the carver thought was the sharp sound of an ax splitting firewood outside.

He considered going to the window to see his father busy reducing heavy chunks of wood to neat manageable pieces that he stacked against the cabin wall close by the door, convenient for his wife. The sounds of woodland birds created a wondrous chorus for the simple tasks of his parents: chattering wrens, burring woodpeckers, and the mysterious liquid trills of a solitary wood thrush.

Suddenly, there was a loud crash. He heard his father yell, and the world went dark. He gradually wakened to a world without light, with only the hushed conversation of his mother and father joined by an unfamiliar male voice. It was the village doctor, called out to attend to a gravely injured adolescent. Father was telling him how the accident happened: he and another woodcutter were felling an ancient oak, notching the massive trunk with their axes, the razor sharp ax heads alternating mechanically as they made chips fly on all sides. They had perfectly calculated the fall line and were just stepping back to watch the immense tree slowly fall to earth, calling out their usual "Timber" as they gazed in awe at the majestic oak's descent. But one of its extended boughs caught a large dead branch snagged high in a nearby tree and the errant deadwood came crashing down, striking the gawking boy on the back of his head.

The waking boy heard the doctor say how lucky he was to be alive. He was encouraged by the young man's responses to questions: he seemed to still have his wits about him and could move his limbs on command. Only gradually did anyone realize that the boy couldn't see anything. The youth felt the first overwhelming sense of having lost so much of the world forever.

Even in his dream, the woodcarver relived the anguish of that realization. Already as a boy he had taken such unspeakable delight in the beauty of the world: though he lived in a small world, working with his father in the great woods, every season and each day brought him endless delight. He knew every species of tree and bush, every bird, insect, and animal. He knew the great swings of the seasons and the subtle moods of the day. Even as he did the laborious tasks of a woodcutter's apprentice, he was encompassed by a magical world of recurrence and unexpected variety.

As he gradually accepted his blindness, the boy was glad for the heightened vividness of his other perceptions: now the fragrance of wildflowers evoked their forms and colors more powerfully than ever; the sounds of wind roaring in the bare winter woods or caressing the soft new leaves of spring, evoked compelling visual images. But still he grieved at the thin reality of these images, arising from mere memory or imagination, not from the rich dense beauty of nature itself.

Now he was moving back and forth between absorbing dreams and memories, and reflections on them, still wavering between sleep and waking. He saw himself working beside his father again, unable to do some of the tasks he had done before, but refining his skills at honing the axes, stacking the split pieces, and other work his father needed done. As he put small limbs and branches onto piles to be used for kindling or burnt for wood ash, he began to find interesting forms. His fingers traced the bend of pliant branches and he sensed how they could be woven into useful things, like hoops for buckets and children's toys, shaped into handles for doors and lids, or whittled into figures of people and animals. Now, at the end of a day of work in the woods, he would have a trove of wooden remnants to carry home. It pleased his parents to see him so involved in creating a marvelous array of devices, toys, and figures as they sat quietly at night, the dark cabin illuminated only by the flickering fireplace.

He had a vivid recollection of the first time anyone from outside saw and praised his creations. The man was an itinerant merchant who sold staples to the forest dwellers: tin ware, fabrics, pins and needles, spices, and other necessary or playful items. When the peddler saw the boy's collection of wild animals, little human forms and odd wooden puzzles, he was excited and immediately thought of ways to sell these in his travels to villages and towns. After that, the boy increased his efforts to imagine new things to carve or shape, and he eagerly built up a supply to sell to the merchant. It gave him great satisfaction to contribute to his family's meager earnings in this way.

As he grew up and gained creative skill he began to work with larger pieces of wood: not just twigs and branches, but stout limbs and, eventually, the massive trunks of trees. When the merchant came around they bartered carefully: the youth obtaining chisels, draw knives, files, and other cutting tools in exchange for carved figures that were becoming more ambitious and substantial with each visit.

At a town market the merchant met a churchman who was struck by the figure of an angel, almost human sized. It revealed the carver's uncanny ability to sense the natural flow and grain of the wood he worked with: using the fork of a tree for the widespread wings and the arc of the trunk for a torso that seemed perfectly alive. On the spot, the churchman purchased the angel and commissioned three similar angelic forms to stand at the entrance to his chapel.

Following that ambitious quartet of angels came a surge of requests for other forms: a school wanted full scale animal figures for its playground that the children could play on but also learn from; a courthouse ordered a bold large lion to stand in the open foyer at the entrance to the court; wealthy families sought curious gnomes and faeries for their gardens.

That began a major shift in the woodcarver's work. Now his father took his son along in the woods to search for just the right trees. The youth would describe the forms he needed and his father and helpers kept their eyes open for them. When they led him to promising trees, they marveled at how his hands moved so searchingly over the trunks and limbs before saying what to cut free and what to leave behind.

By then they had constructed a studio close to the cabin as a workshop for the carver. It had a long sturdy bench able to support large pieces of wood and set in the middle of the shop so he could move freely around it as he gradually unfolded the living forms he sought. All his tools were arrayed on pegs on the wall, each just where he could find it ready to hand. A storage area at the back held works waiting for the merchant, and outside, under a slanted roof, an odd assortment of stock material was carefully arranged in readiness for their transformation.

It was in that time that the woodcarver first met the girl who would become the heart of his life, the light of his world. She was just passing from innocence to womanhood, the eldest daughter of a woodsman who worked with the carver's father. When her brother left the forest to find his way in a nearby village, she eagerly volunteered to take his place on the woods crew. Of course, she would not do the heavy or dangerous work of her older brother; but she could fetch water from streams, keep the axes sharp, gather small limbs into piles for burning, and perform many other such tasks.

Until then the carver was rarely in the presence of any female other than his mother. Sometimes travelers stopped on their journey through the great woods, seeking food and drink at the isolated cabin. The carver would listen to the children playing and the elders talking, but he remained withdrawn. Everyone assumed he would always stay in his parents' home and be cared for by his mother.

But now each time he went along with the woods crew he encountered the girl. Both were shy and worked with few words; but their work brought them together often as the girl described promising trees and branches and guided him to them. She had a fascination with unusual shapes and textures as well, and before long they felt a deep kinship in seeking mysteries the forest hid from others. Sometimes they would be off alone together, sharing a lunch the girl made for them and speaking about the wonders of this wooded world.

When the woodcarver's mother fell ill, it became apparent that the two men were hardly able to take over much of her necessary work. The father's friend offered the help of his daughter until Mother was well again. At first the girl came on days needing her special help—doing laundry, preserving produce from their garden, sewing new clothes. But, as Mother worsened, the maiden offered to stay through the week, leaving her younger sisters to help at home. So, they cleared a small space at the back of the cabin for her sleep and privacy, and the maiden moved in with them.

Now she often stayed home from the sojourns into the woods, caring for the failing mother, serving as cook and seamstress and keeper of the home fires. The carver missed her help and presence when he was off with the woods crew, but he returned home eagerly with the thought of being close to her again. In the evening she would sometimes read from books of poetry and old stories for him, and they entered further into a separate world.

One evening, as they sat close by the open fire talking about a story the maiden had just read, she noticed a cut on his hand. All the woodsmen had to take special care of their hands, working each day with rough wood and sharp cutting tools. So, the women had long ago learned to find herbs and other forest materials for making ointments to soften calluses, balms for cuts and abrasions, and coatings to protect men's hands from the biting cold of winter. The maiden went to Mother's cupboard for the balm she kept there. Holding the woodcarver's large rough hand, she lovingly anointed the wound. Then she used Mother's lotion to soften both hands. As she gently massaged each finger and rubbed the smooth fragrant cream into the powerful hands, they both felt a thrill of intimacy pass through them. The maiden asked whether his fingers still had the sensitivity of his youth: the carver confessed that working so long had toughened his hands a great deal. They had become much stronger and able to resist slivers and nicks, as if they were leather gloves. But he was losing his ability to feel the delicate nuances of the woods he worked on, especially when he carved small or intricate figures.

Immediately, the maiden resolved to find a remedy for his fading sense of touch. The next time she went home, she questioned her mother: was there some concoction of natural remedies that could restore or even heighten the sense of touch? Her mother had some ideas, and together they went to the cabin of a solitary old woman, wise in the ways of cures, for her counsel. She knew of several ways to waken touch and already had most of the ingredients in her stock of dried pods and flowers, rare fragrant roots, and small containers of extracts. By chance, the season was just right to find the few fresh items also needed. Excitedly, three generations of forest women combined their skill and care to prepare the special lotion.

That very evening, after their dinner, the maiden told everyone about the new remedy she had found. Sitting by the fire again, she took the carver's hands in her small delicate hands and began coating them with a fragrant film of lotion. Although the parents sat beside them watching, the maiden and carver seemed in a separate world as he gave her his workman's hands and she caressed and anointed them.

This treatment became a nightly ritual, part of the maiden's reading for the carver. Slowly, but perceptibly, the carver felt his fingertips return to their youthful sensitivity. In the studio he allowed himself to work again on small delicate figures, even going beyond anything he had done before. It was almost like regaining his vision.

Months later, when Mother died suddenly and peacefully, it seemed a foregone conclusion that the maiden would remain in the household. Her position brought a small compensation for her parents and they saw hope in her moving a little way from their care and into a safe familiar world. For herself, all of this seemed like a natural extension of her young life. She had vague dreams about a larger life, one that would bring more than stories and mere imaginings to her; but she was also hesitant to leave the only world she had ever known and dearly loved.

And she was growing ever closer to the woodcarver. He was nearly twenty years her senior, but still had a boyish spirit and a heart so like her own. Living under the same roof with him, sharing all the moods and tasks of each day, she felt almost like a younger sister—certainly not a mere servant. There were daily chances for casual talk and the sharing of simple silences.

Often, when Father was away in the forest and the carver remained at home to work, the maiden would go out to the studio with tea and some small baked delicacy. He would stop his work and sit with her. He loved to have her tell him about features of the wood he couldn't see—colors, stains, patterns of line and visual texture. Of course, she found all his work wonderful; so intuitive and often unexpected, even when she had helped him select the stock and heard some of his intentions.

The carver loved to share his work this way and to have someone who genuinely understood his creative mind. He told her that true beauty cannot be forced, nor is it the simple product of mere planning and mechanical execution. The final figure is not already present in the stock, just waiting for the sculptor to remove the excess, like breaking a casting mold; but neither is it present in the blueprint of his mind, just needing some passive medium to give it substance. The crouching panther, ascending angel, or kneeling gnome are the spontaneous interplay between medium and mind. The artist doesn't simply find the form, nor does he create it out of thin air. It's like the new being that magically arises when lovers find each other.

In sharing such intimate conversations, alone together, they found each other. Sitting close to the carver one afternoon, her mind utterly absorbed in his reflective words and the powerful presence of his current project, the maiden began to weep. She wasn't sad or frightened, but she didn't understand what was opening in her and making her tremble so powerfully and mysteriously. He heard her gentle sobbing and she saw his attentive concern and reached out for his extended hand. Then they were embracing and weeping together, their wet cheeks pressed close as they spoke beautiful unintelligible words that seemed to come from one voice. They began kissing each other, comforting and cleansing each other as their lips explored each other's face. The carver held the maiden's face in his sensitive hands and he saw her clearly for the first time. He traced every feature of her beautiful face, telling her how perfect she was in every detail as his delicate fingertips moved over her from brow to chin. When his fingers touched her full soft lips she kissed them and told him how beautiful he was as well. Then they kissed and could not stop for a long time, inhaling each other's warm breath, tasting each other's words of love.

Until that moment, neither had realized how powerfully they were being drawn together. But, in that moment, there was an infallible realization of their utter oneness. After they regained some composure, the pair talked freely about everything that seemed wonderful about their world and how much they could become in it together.

When Father came home from a long day in the forest, he immediately sensed the new intimacy between his son and the maiden. She had prepared their evening meal as usual, but she seemed so focused on the blind man, so attentive to his simplest words.

The old man remembered his own early love, when he and his wife first married and became real forest dwellers. He was just now emerging from the swamp of grief that engulfed him with his wife's sudden decline and death. Having the maiden in their home, taking care of all the domestic tasks, seemed like a continuation of his wife's presence. She both lightened his sorrow and deepened it. To see his son and the maiden draw close to each other gladdened his heart and gave him new hope for his son's future. But he yearned to be with his departed wife again.

In the following months, the carver and the maiden deepened their bond. When they accompanied the father and woods crew into the forest, they did almost every task together. In their free time, the maiden led the carver to her favorite places, especially in search of herbs and roots and various forest edibles. This was a part of forest life and lore that had been invisible to the carver, the world of women's perception and understanding. The maiden had learned this from her own mother and other women wise in the ways of the forest. The carver was like a child discovering new mysteries, and she loved to be his tutor. Often, in addition to materials they gathered for his sculpture, they brought home baskets with mushrooms, sassafras roots and herbs for medicine and cooking.

When they stayed at home, the carver worked with new energy and vision, preferring spontaneous sculptural ideas to the items others commissioned or that were his routine productions. The maiden joined him in the studio more often and worked closely with him in selecting stock and helping him discover the unique potentialities of each piece. They lingered over tea and delicacies from her stove as their conversations about nature and art wove them ever closer into a single fabric.

Then one day, just as the carver was beginning his nap, a frantic beating at the door roused them. It was a boy from the woods crew, sweating and shaking. The carver's father had collapsed in mid stroke as he hewed a long log. He was dead immediately, probably of a failed heart. They hurried to the site and knew the terrible truth of it. The carver knelt by his father's sprawled body and he wept profoundly as his hands moved over the old man's face and upper body.

According to forest custom, he was buried the next day in a simple grave in the cabin yard, lying in peace beside his wife of many years. A small group of forest dwellers joined the circle, sharing their grief and gratitude with a few plain words and their unshakeable presence.

Like many other small communities around the world and throughout history, these forest dwellers lived in harmony with their natural setting and with each other. Each person was nested in a family and a circle of families. When their needs reached beyond such intimate circles, they were supported by others living a common life. To build a substantial cabin requires many hands and skills; to carry on a business of logging and sawing timber and providing firewood for nearby villagers requires the dependable coordination of many men and women. The birthing of children, the provision of draft animals and feed crops, the demands of storms and destructive fires need the shared efforts of a whole web of forest people.

On the day of the burial, the woodcarver felt his place within that web with special gratitude. In less than a year he had lost his mother, the heart and hands of their home, and his father, their source of income and engagement with the wider world. The maiden had somewhat replaced his mother. Now, he would need to somehow stand for his father in their continuing life.

He had vaguely presumed that one day he would be joined in marriage with the maiden and that they would continue the way of life so securely grounded in this cabin, this place, this circle of friends and fellow workers. Now he felt free to invite the maiden to his bed, and their intimacies became more spontaneous and open than they could be before. Until then, they didn't allow themselves to think beyond the immediate demands of their world, living with Mother and Father and then with Father alone. They just accepted that as their circumstance.

Now they were forced to face what their new situation would allow or require of them. There was no need to marry, but it was the common way for a man and a woman to share a life. And the power of their love made them yearn for an ever deeper union, with every aspect of their lives woven into a single seamless garment, or integrated organically into one body, one life.

For the woodcarver this vision was easy, since he had experienced such a life with his parents and could imagine no higher life than the one he was settled in. His blindness made other options seem impossible, so he never considered life beyond the forest, exploring the world of cities and higher culture.

But for the maiden, even in the security and serenity of the carver's embrace and her satisfactions with her place in their simple life, the lure of a wider world and unknown possibilities was still alive. When her brother returned from that world, his stories intrigued her: he had seen things and encountered people almost unimaginable in the forest. And when the world came to the cabin doorstep, she often felt wonder and envy.

A vivid instance was the periodic visits by travelling merchants and tradesmen. Tin smiths, garment dealers, and tradesmen of many kinds passed through the forest, meeting the special needs of these isolated people and stirring up their desires for unexpected things. Some offered books and pictures; some were story tellers; some were visionaries trying to lure people to their cause or way. One of those visitors had been the old merchant who first opened the world of grand sculpture to the carver.

In recent years, the merchant's son had taken his place. He continued to come to the forest every few months, offering a wide assortment of useful and entertaining items. He was now the carver's main link to markets for his work. The maiden had waited for him with special excitement. He was still young, handsome and so full of life. The world he opened to her with his engaging tales seemed so wonderful that she was always left afterwards with a vague longing to follow him into it.

But once she settled into the woodsmen's cabin, and especially now that she had found a magical union with the carver, she laughed at herself for such idle daydreams, and even felt guilt at indulging them in any way.

Then, in this mild spring afternoon, the maiden was brought to an unexpected but fateful moment. The dog barked softly and she heard the creaking of the young merchant's cart stopping at the gate. She checked the sleeping carver to be sure he was comfortable, and hurried outside. In the charming presence of the merchant, she was again caught up in considering his new merchandise and listening to the delightful stories he offered her. Standing on the inside of the gate, she had him bring samples of intriguing items for her examination and she felt a surge of excitement at the young man's closeness.

It was then that the woodcarver was slowly wakened: first by the moist nose of his dog nuzzling against his face, and then by the dim sounds of two voices from the window. Sleepily, he rose from the bed and felt his way to the open window. He heard his beloved's musical voice and then recognized the voice of the young merchant, so reminiscent of his father's in accent and tone. He could not hear exactly what they were saying, but he gathered it was some playful discussion of goods and prices. It was good to hear the maiden so happy in the presence of outsiders.

There must have been some haste in his motion, because he absent-mindedly forgot about a wooden peg temporarily inserted close to the window as a place to hang drying spring herbs. Leaning to the window, he struck his forehead against the peg and was momentarily stunned. He shook his head and mumbled a rebuke for his carelessness.

As if a thick cloud was lifting before him, the carver began to perceive dim but swelling light. He was so accustomed to imagining the old familiar world around him that, at first, he thought this was just an unusually intense recollection of the cabin yard. But now the fog was evaporating more and he could make out the chickens scratching in the grass, the rail fence, and then the gate. There stood the maiden with her back to him, wearing a simple print dress and white apron. She was leaning over the gate, absorbed in examining something held by the merchant. He was bending toward her and their words seemed to become more quiet and private. When the exchange was made, the maiden taking a few towels and the merchant pocketing a coin, the man put his hand on the maiden's arm and brought his face even closer. Abruptly, he kissed her on the cheek and gestured to the dirt road.

The woodcarver was already dazed by the sudden opening of the dark room of his blindness. But the sight of his beloved being enticed by the young merchant stunned him. He felt ashamed to be almost spying on them, and wanted to turn away — wanted never to have seen this momentary scene at all.

Just as the carver started to draw back from the open window, the merchant looked in his direction and the maiden turned her head, following his gaze. For the only time in his life, the woodcarver saw his beloved's face. She was radiant and beautiful beyond anything his knowing fingertips could ever have revealed. Her eyes were the pure deep blue of the small lakes in the forest. Her skin was as white as linden wood and had an inner glow. Her golden hair framed her face exquisitely and tumbled below her shoulders. He longed to gaze at that beauty forever, like an inexhaustible well-spring.

But he immediately realized that he did not want the maiden to know that he had seen her this way, hesitating between their life of promise and some unknown possibilities. So, he pretended to be just standing there unseeing, breathing the fresh spring air. The dog had run into the yard to chase the chickens and snoop at the gate with his tail wagging . The carver called the dog, as if he was unaware of anyone else in the yard. The dog whirled around and dashed back into the cabin.

Even as he returned to the daybed, the world was fading from the carver's eyes. Those few minutes had been so unspeakably delicious and yet so tormenting that he did not resist as his blindness overtook him. He didn't want to ever impose his love upon the maiden, to make her feel entrapped in his adoration and longing. So, he had to return to the cavern of his loneliness and hope for the beloved's return.

When the maiden entered the cabin, she came to the daybed and stood silently over the carver, who feigned sleep. Then she put a kettle on the stove and prepared an early tea break. When the carver stirred and got up, she called him to the table already spread for him. Handing the carver the towels she had purchased, she explained that the merchant had passed through. Then she repeated a funny story he told her, about some children in the village mistaking one of the carver's wooden animals for an actual wild bear loose near their school. The carver chuckled, and they both smiled and relaxed.

Soon it was time for the carver to go to his studio. He was working on a new project about which he had been unusually secretive. The maiden knew he needed a log large enough to yield a life-sized figure of a kneeling person. The grain should follow a certain sinuous line and the wood needed to be golden in color and able to take a very smooth finish. He had carefully covered the work with a canvas each time the maiden came to the studio, telling her it might be a surprise for her. Each time she tried to guess, wondering who might have commissioned the piece or what new idea he was exploring. Perhaps a forest saint or a wood spirit? But he had been playfully evasive.

Since they had enjoyed their tea break earlier than usual, the maiden didn't come out to the studio this afternoon, even though the carver lingered before coming in for dinner. Although the days were staying light and warm later, they went to bed early. The maiden laid beside her friend and lover with her back to him; he curved his body to hers and gently caressed her with his knowing hands as if unveiling a mysterious form. The maiden shuddered and almost swooned with a profound sense of his deep love of her. It was a moment at once erotic and spiritually intimate. Neither spoke as they lay breathing deeply in unison, curved together almost like twins in a womb. Then they sank into a blissful slumber, leaving the difficulties of this day behind on the shores of the fading world.

The next day returned to normal, with the woodcarver working in his studio later than usual. Just before dinner the maiden's brother arrived unexpected. There was a joyful reunion as the girl arranged the table for three. The carver felt almost like an older brother to the young man. They had worked together in the forest for many years, and the maiden had recounted so many of his stories about life in the world that they both felt as if they too had ventured there.

While the maiden cleared the table and washed dishes, the carver led the youth outside to describe a small construction project he needed help with. He knew the youth sometimes worked as a carpenter in town, and was sure he had all the skills needed. By the time the maiden came out to see what they were doing, the men had already plotted the outlines for a small six-sided structure and agreed on all the materials required to realize the carver's vision. When the youth left for his family's cabin, they had arranged to begin the building project in two days.

Now the maiden was really curious about what the carver was up to. She teased him and prodded him for some clue, but without success. She wondered whether the structure had to do with the mysterious figure he was carving so secretively. In bed that night they moved from playful teasing like children to passionate love making.

The next day, the carver went to the studio very early and barely took a break for lunch. He skipped his usual nap and worked until the maiden had to call him repeatedly for dinner. She could tell from the golden dust on his upper body that he had reached the sanding stage of his work, so he must be close to completion. Ordinarily it was she who did the final filing and sanding, choosing just the right oils to stain or preserve the wood. But, on this occasion he wanted to do the entire process by himself.

On the following day, before breakfast, the brother arrived with a horse-drawn wagon, filled with wooden materials, which they quickly unloaded. Six solid peeled posts for the vertical supports, rough hewn planks for the base, smaller straight branches for enclosing rails, timbers for cross pieces to support the floor and roof, and a stack of shaved cedar shingles to keep the roof boards water tight. There were even six large flat rocks from a nearby river to serve as foundation stones.

They hurriedly ate breakfast, with the maiden gradually getting a better picture of what they were going to construct. It was going to be a viewing pavilion designed to hold the mysterious figure on a low pedestal. The pavilion would be located midway between the cabin and the studio, close to the stone path connecting them.

The construction went smoothly, due to the careful design of the carver and the skilled carpentry of the youth. By lunch, the six posts rose from their stone bases, locked together with solid joists above and below. Part of the floor was already put down, making the structure even more solid. The maiden had never seen the carver building a structure, and she was pleased with his amazing skills and the joy he took in the work.

Soon they were back at the task, finishing the floor and turning to the latticed rails enclosing it. A small swinging gate and a single stone step provided entrance. The brother had brought a short ladder, and he now climbed onto the upper structure and began raising the roof timbers. Around that base he arranged ceiling boards carefully sawed so they locked everything together.

The woodcarver was so eager to complete their project that they barely paused for a light dinner, agreeing to have a celebratory meal when the job was done. Then the youth was kneeling on the roof nailing down cedar shingles that the carver passed up to him from the ladder. The maiden helped by carrying small bundles of shingles to them. The late sun allowed them to complete the project with time and daylight enough to clean up remnants and tools and place them in the wagon.

After a simple dinner, they sat on the back step of the cabin enjoying fresh strawberries and delicate cake the maiden had prepared. Brother and sister wanted to describe the pavilion to the carver but, before they could begin, he did so himself. Gesturing as if he could see the completed structure outlined against the glowing western sky, he led them on an imaginary walk around the pavilion and then into its small space. They were all wonderfully pleased with what they had done together. But what exactly was that?

Like a child planning a big secret for his mother, the carver sent the maiden inside, telling her not to peek while he and her brother moved his sculpture to the pavilion. It didn't take long, and she listened at the door as they whispered and groaned with their efforts. There was a big cheer at their success, and the two men came in. Still, neither one would say a word about what they had just done. When the brother finally left for home, the men hugged like comrades sharing a mission.

The carver told the maiden she would need to contain her curiosity just a little longer, until daybreak. He held her simply and peacefully, gently kissing her eyes and whispering words of love. Soon the weary man sank smoothly into deep sleep, like a green log disappearing into a river's dark waters when loggers slide it down for transport to the mill.

The maiden was restive through the night and, even before the rooster started to crow, her eyes were wide open, looking for the first traces of dawn at the window. Finally, she just had to get out of bed, careful not to disturb the carver, and quietly begin the first tasks of the day: putting kindling in the stove, starting a snapping flame, and setting a kettle to heat water. She assumed that they would go out to the pavilion after breakfast; but, even before she could begin heating the frying pan for pancakes, she heard the carver climbing out of bed. He came up behind her in his night shirt and embraced her, nuzzling against her neck and burying his face in her long loose golden hair. He said "Good morning my dear love," and asked her to pour hot water for a pot of tea to take out with them.

It was going to be a clear bright day, but night was still lingering under the surrounding trees. In the dim light the maiden could barely see a golden form inside the pavilion. As they approached, she held a basket with the tea pot and cups in her right hand and the carver took the other in his gentle powerful hand. He reached forward and swung the gate open, inviting the maiden to go first.

The sun was just emerging through the dark trees, sending shafts of golden light into the yard. The maiden's eyes widened in wonder as she saw the mysterious figure. It was a woman, kneeling so that she sat back on her legs and leaned forward with extended arms. Her head was tilted upward and the sunlight illumined the beautiful lines of her face and flowing hair.

The maiden was so taken that the basket almost fell from her grip. She turned to the carver just as he began to speak: "I call her 'The Lady of Light.' She is my tribute to you, my dearest one. You have given me the world in ways I never dreamed possible. She stands between our cabin and the studio, between domesticity and art, just as you are an angel bearing precious gifts back and forth between the centers of our shared life." He paused, as if searching for more, but was interrupted by her passionate embrace and her lips on his.

When they separated and the maiden caught her breath, she said, "O my dear man, you are too wonderful for me. I have to tell you of a dream I had last night. It was a beautiful autumn day, with brilliant leaves drifting down all around our cabin. All our friends were gathered in our yard, encircling us. I was wearing a pure white dress for you and for our wedding. The village priest was there and then we swore our vows. My dearest friend, let me be your wife forever." They embraced again, weeping in unspeakable joy in each other's arms. The carver began kissing the tears from the maiden's lovely face. and she wiped his away with her delicate hands. "Dear lady, you have read my heartagain. This figure is my adoration of you, and I was just about to ask for your hand in marriage. I never dreamed I could have anything more than each glorious day I share with you. But now I know we can have the rest of our life together in this place, in this beautiful way."

That day the woodcarver did not work in his studio. After lingering at breakfast, they spent the morning in intimate play. The carver carried in buckets of water from the well and together they heated a small tubful. Then they undressed each other and the carver bathed his beloved, his caring yearning hands moving over her wet smooth body, far more wonderful than that of the wooden lady. After he had thoroughly dried her with a soft warm towel, the maiden bathed the carver. His upper body was so powerful, from many years using mallets and cutting tools. As her hands cleansed every part of his sculpted body, her kisses followed after them. Then she took his hand and led him to their bed.

Later, in the warm afternoon, they strolled in the nearby forest. The maiden carried a basket for gathering herbs and flowers to set on their table. She had taught the carver every flower and herb, and she delighted in testing him by holding each treasure to his face so he could distinguish them by fragrance or texture. As they moved among the ancient trees, they began to plan their wedding day.

The maiden's dream was the richest source of ideas for their wedding. It was set in early autumn, after everyone's garden had been harvested and prepared for winter. There was an abundance of squash, beans, fresh greens, potatoes, and other produce. The custom of their people was for the wedding guests to prepare a feast, each family bringing their contribution to the wedding. The maiden's mother made a special dress for her, and the maiden sewed a white, bloused shirt and new trousers for the carver. The bride's family arranged invitations for guests and asked the local priest to preside. The maiden gathered flowers from her garden and the surrounding forest to make garlands.

When guests began to arrive, on foot or in small carts, they found the gate swung open to them and festooned with a colorful garland. Soon the priest joined them and, after a few greetings, gathered the group into a small circle. After a short reading from "The Song of Songs," the priest asked for an exchange of symbols of their undying love. The maiden's sisters stepped forward, each holding a beautiful floral crown made of the same elements as the gate's garland. The carver hadn't expected this, so the maiden explained her meaning. "My dear love, let these living circles of beauty signify our mutual love. In each year and every season, let us find the beauty of the forest and wind it into such radiant rings to testify to our devotion." The woodcarver's hands trembled as he placed a crown of flowers on his beloved's head, and he bent down for her to do the same for him. Everyone was profoundly silent as this rite was followed by the exchange of simple but eternal promises, and the woodcarver and the maiden were joined in marriage. A loud cheer went up from the circle of friends.

Then the woodcarver raised his arms to call for silence. "My dear friends, we thank you all for sharing this rare moment with us. We thank you for every form of kind help you have given us and our families for so long and for this day. We ask for your continuing love as we begin a new life among you, even as we promise to continue as your loving neighbors. Now let us join in sharing the wonderful feast which you have provided."

The meal was brought out into the yard, with each person serving others. The day was awash in warm autumnal light and a gentle breeze carried forest fragrances to them. Friendly jests and stories were passed around like small gifts. Someone commented that the chickens must be jealous, having to be cooped up from their yard. Someone else went inside and let the eager dog out to join the party. There was cider to drink and many toasts to the new couple and to the whole gathering.

When everyone was finished eating and things were cleaned up, the carver led the group into the back yard. They had never seen a pavilion before and everyone began exclaiming about its beauty, astounded that mere stones and wood from the forest could be shaped into such a structure. The encircling rail was wreathed in a floral garland. The carver credited his new brother with most of the skill in construction. Then he opened the gate and invited small groups to step inside as everyone else clustered around and peered in.

Of course, they all knew of his work, but none had ever seen the larger pieces of sculpture which were carried to the village and surrounding towns on the merchant's cart. Now they were amazed by the lifelike figure, and immediately saw the maiden embodied in the golden form: the outlines of her young body under a loose garment, her long flowing hair spilling down her back, and the finest details of her beautiful face. After all had a chance to see the figure up close, the carver announced that her name was "My Lady of Light." Everyone understood some of his meaning, and they joined in applause for the new couple.

For the rest of the afternoon, people strolled around the cabin and grounds, talking in small groups. Each couple found a private moment to visit the parents' grave site. Everyone was curious about the studio, with its collection of tools and works in progress. The carver presented each child with one of his whimsical wooden toys. The old folks walked through the garden, comparing it to their own and discussing the year's growing season. The women got a casual tour inside the cabin, while the children romped in spontaneous games.

As dusk approached, only the maiden's family remained, helping with final clean up and silently enjoying this new extension of their world. When they left as well, the new couple was finally alone in their transformed world. Hand in hand, they went to where Mother and Father rested, lingering to share their joy and feel the presence of the man and woman who had created this forest haven for them.

The maiden suggested that her husband check to be sure everything was left in order in the yard and his studio while she went inside. When he came in, they embraced and exchanged their first private words of love as a newly wedded couple. The maiden asked her husband to sit on the daybed as she slowly undressed for him, telling him how she was unveiling her body for him, step by step. Then she came to him, so glad to give her nakedness to his loving hands. Soon she was undressing him as well and leading him to their bed. The woodcarver could not see what she had prepared for them, but, as soon as they got close, he realized what she had done. She had taken the fragrant garland from their front gate and draped it around their bed. She led his hand to the floral ring and. together, they lifted it aside as they entered their marital bed.

Later, they laid side by side on their backs, exchanging brief soft words amid spells of rich silence. Darkness enfolded them and it seemed as if they were drifting in a small boat on a vast sea, gently rocking on long great swells.

II - Adoration

The Forest Inn nestles securely in a wide bend of the Bow River. Ancient trees surround the low-set log structure, sheltering it from storms that sometimes roll in across the broad river. The Inn was built almost a hundred years ago, offering accommodations to travelers about midway between Mountain View to the north and the capital to the south. In the beginning, the Inn primarily served men connected with the logging business (buyers, sellers and managers) who oversaw the long exploitation of the virgin forests.

With its headwaters in the mountain tops, the Bow was the natural (and only) way to move the massive native logs down to the sawmills closer to the capital. Big Bend was the first point on the river where the rush of mountain streams had gathered enough volume to carry a full raft of logs.

The Great Forest reached from the high coniferous slopes to the mixed timbers on the plateau surrounding Mountain View, to the once dense hardwoods of the foothills which flatten out several miles beyond the Inn. In only a few places could you still find remnants of the once mighty native trees. The Inn was one such place, owing its enclosure of massive oaks, maples and beeches to its early construction and the stubborn resistance of a long line of inn-keepers, who demanded that no axes or cross-cut saws would make a mockery of its name or heritage.

The Inn had its site because of geography and economics. Being the first large pause in the river's rush south, Big Bend was an ideal location for river runners to tie up their huge floats of logs, using the deep eddies and quiet stretches as launching bases for the journey to the mills. Just a couple miles upstream the Bow was swelled by the waters of Crazy Creek, a wild disjointed river descending from the far northeast, full of rapids and falls that made most of it impassable for men in boats and barely practical even for free-floating timber. Only in spring flooding could anyone dare to risk a run of logs down its gorges to the comparative calm of the Bow.

Far to the north, Mountain View had sprung up as a rough logging camp, with a rugged dirt trail its first connection with the capital and other points south. In its early boom days it was a conglomeration of raw wooden shacks for the workers and a few small supporting businesses—a general store, a cheap hotel including a saloon, a barbershop and laundry, and the inevitable bawdy house. Prosperity brought more permanence and refinement, so by the time the logging had to slow down there remained a decent collection of better homes and residents.

On the late autumn evening which we are considering, a traveler coming south to the Inn on the dirt road which parallels the Bow would have experienced a dramatic scene. Most of the hardwoods had shed their wilting leaves, so their bare branches made a tangled screen that partly blocked the brilliant western sky. Deep tones of red and orange smoldered on the horizon like dying coals in an immense open furnace. The flames danced across the river's variegated surface, intensifying as light escaped the shaded western shore and reached the Inn.

A wall of checkered windows facing the river was so ablaze with the sun's departing brilliance that the traveler might momentarily imagine that the Inn itself was on fire. Moving closer, he would have seen the outlines of four figures standing at the windows, gazing out at the brilliant but fading display.

These four men were the Inn's only guests for the night. Each had arrived in the late afternoon, travelling separately and needing the welcome accommodations the Inn offered. Two had arrived in closed carriages, which now stood beside the Inn's stable where the horses and their drivers were housed. Another had come in a light buggy which he handled himself. The last guest had come on horseback, passing his tired stallion to the stable hand before striding to the Inn's entrance.

The innkeeper had greeted his guests with traditional hospitality, registering each man while making discreet inquiries about their day's travels. All four had started from different directions, with three converging near the Inn from the northern mountains and one heading north into higher elevations.

After they settled into their small comfortable rooms, the men cleaned up from the sweat and dust of their day's travel. When the dinner bell sounded through the Inn, the men descended to the dining room where the innkeeper and his wife had laid out a generous array of country fare. A large pork roast filled a platter, with bowls of steamed potatoes and carrots on either side. A substantial loaf of brown bread rested on a cutting board, partially sliced and still exuding heat from just having been baked. Each place at the table had a tankard of ale which, as the keeper explained proudly and fulsomely, was made at the Inn itself from a recipe tracing back to the Inn's founder.

The men were famished from their long journeys and were just about to fill their plates when the inn keeper gestured for their attention. "Here at Forest Inn we have learned over many years that it's good to follow a simple procedure for helping our guests get acquainted while enjoying their dinner. I understand that each of you is unknown to the others, so first you need to get acquainted. Let's use this dinner as a time to become familiar with each other. Give us a good sense of who you are: where is your home. What is your work? What are some of your broad thoughts on your life? I suggest beginning at the head of the table and moving around to the left, as in playing a game of cards. You can be as brief or expansive as you choose, but from past experience I know that after a first circuit you will be prompted to fill out your initial remarks by your table companions' comments. That should be more than enough to occupy you over dinner."

"Then we can retire to the fireplace for relaxation, coffee and dessert, and the second part of your conversation. Having heard some of your life story and situation, we will all be curious about what recent journey has brought you together just for this evening."

The men readily agreed, especially since they were strangers to one another and, in varying ways, unsure what protocol to follow. As the meal began, the guest at the head of the table introduced himself. His stout figure and rather formal attire showed the middle-aged man to be of a higher class. He explained that he was a business man, born and raised in the capital, a second generation buyer and seller of many kinds of merchandise. His work required that he travel widely, always seeking profitable ways to match producers with those who used or merchandized their goods. He did not himself sell directly to individual users, though he carried a large inventory of samples of the goods he wholesaled. Perhaps the other men would be interested in coming to his room afterwards to look at some of his inventory.

Although he missed his wife and children, and was eager to return to their good life in the city, he treasured these extended trips into the surrounding districts. As a young man he had often joined his father in his business travels, continuing his father's associations with clients and friends in often far-flung regions of the country. Because he dealt with a wide variety of goods and served as a go-between for such diverse sellers and buyers, he had acquired a rich sense of the people of this land and their many enterprises.

After sharing anecdotes about how he learned his father's trade and some of his experiences as a travelling wholesaler, the business man passed the speaker's role to the small elderly man on his left. His black garments and clerical collar made it evident that he was a man of the Church. He told the others that he was a priest, recently retired from parish work and now serving at the Bishop's will. His long acquaintance with the Franciscan order made him especially qualified to work as an envoy to the small groups of Franciscan brothers and sisters working throughout the diocese. So he, too, now had to travel quite widely in this part of the world, not buying and selling but helping the Bishop stay informed about the diverse ways agents of the Church labored in the vineyards. And, in gathering many kinds of information, the cleric also carried directives from the Bishop to parishes and religious communities.

The old priest was soft-spoken and of a serene disposition, so that the other guests had to lean toward him to catch his words over the crackling in the fire-place. He ended his story without having said much about himself and what had drawn him to the priesthood: perhaps more of that would come out when he told of his most recent travels. When he paused, the group waited expectantly for a fuller story. But the priest simply gestured to the old man beside him, inviting him to pick up the circle of tales.

This man had the manner and dress of a scholar, with small eye-glasses and a way of squinting at things that suggested both a lively curiosity and some difficulty in seeing things clearly. As he began, he explained that, unlike the first speakers, he was not an agent for some larger enterprise, whether business or church, but a man whose hobby had become his passion. He was a shop-keeper in a small southern village, specializing in rare books and the products of regional artists and craftsmen. His work brought him into close associations with many people in his area. That's what started his interest in the local history of small communities. Since his shop specialized in traditional arts and crafts, he naturally began his studies by visiting the little communities or settlements of people who supplied his shop with their wares. Especially during times when his business was quiet, he would hitch his old mare to his buggy and journey to villages which supplied him. He would return, not only with new items to stock his shelves, but with his notebooks stuffed with information and stories about the history and life of those villages. His presence at the Inn was just the result of such a mixed venture.

People who knew of his interest in social history and traditional craftsmanship encouraged him to write a collection of essays that would gather many of his observations and perhaps comprise a guidebook to some of the out-of-the-way settlements that still preserved much of the country's earlier ways.

Each guest had paced his remarks to allow for the passing of dishes and the leisurely consumption of the abundant food The keeper oversaw the meal, refilling tankards and retreating to the kitchen to assist his cheerful wife in bringing additional bowls and platters to the table. Thick candles illuminated the table and the keeper kept the large fireplace supplied with wood that provided waves of warmth and dancing light.

As the meal drew to a close, it was time for the final guest to speak about himself. Unlike the others, he was a young man, making his first venture into the northern mountain country. He was a recent graduate of the university in the capital, having specialized in the study of mythology and folklore. His particular interest was in tales about creative and inspiring individuals. People (fictional or real) who seemed almost superhuman in their visions and talents, so that others were drawn to them and challenged to achievements and transformations they would otherwise never have imagined possible. The young man shared a couple stories that illustrated his interests and explained how he himself had been drawn into his subject.

As the Inn keeper had predicted, the guests had all been intrigued by each other's personal stories and were eager to learn how these related to the ways they had been carried to just this place at this time. After a short session of questions and comments, the keeper guided the group to the comfortable chairs arranged in front of the huge stone fireplace. By then the crackling flames had died down enough to allow for easy conversation. The keeper and his wife brought out a generous pot of coffee and a platter stacked with freshly baked tarts filled with apple slices, flavored with sugar and cinnamon, and topped with walnut halves. As the guests savored the desserts and complimented the keeper's wife, she explained modestly that the tarts were from an old Inn recipe just for this season, using apples from their own small orchard and walnuts gathered from an ancient tree close to the river.

The keeper saw that his guests were beginning to settle deeply into their chairs and the cozy atmosphere of the room. He tapped his cup with a fork. "My dear guests, now that we have heard a little about your personal stories, it's time to hear about your most recent travels and how they brought us together on this autumnal evening. May I suggest that we follow the order that worked so well over dinner. As we proceed, it would be my honor to serve you some of the brandy that has been made especially for the Inn for nearly a century by a small monastery in the mountains."

Taking this cue, the merchant shifted his chair to face his fellow travelers and began. "Well, as I have already said, I was born to the buying and selling trade. Since I neither produce the wares I sell nor sell directly to the final users of my goods, I need to travel as a go-between. It isn't always a comfortable life, with so much time spent on the road away from my dear wife and children. But it is a way with familiar rhythms which renews old acquaintances in predictable patterns. So, though I don't get to Mountain View more than once in three years, I always make sure to complete this leg of my travels before winter storms come. And I always look forward to the luscious fare and kind company of this Inn."

"Mountain View still has the roughness you would expect from an old logging town. But each year it is becoming more refined, so there are new markets for finery in clothes, fashion in furnishings, books by modern authors, and many more items that I can supply. I just spent several days there renewing contacts with buyers I have dealt with since my father's time. Transporting goods to and from Mountain View is still a problem because of the poor road and long winters, but each year they are shipping more south and returning with products from the capital and elsewhere. I am lucky to be right in the middle of all this growth."

"One day, a good friend who has a small furniture business took me to a place further up the mountain than I had been before. He told me it was a new convent that was celebrating some special dedication just then. On the rough ride up to the convent he gave me some background on the religious community. Though it had been founded only a few years ago and was quite small (he thought about a dozen nuns), they already had a beautiful chapel and an attached cloister. I could see that as we drew near, the convent set on a green forested shelf just below a great wall of grey rock. Both buildings were made from hewn logs, very substantial and surprisingly beautiful, their golden wood glowing in the sunlight. The chapel is narrow but over two stories high, with a modest spire above the altar area. When we entered I expected great darkness, but the shutters on the high slender windows were open, allowing shafts of brilliant light to slant through, just like you sometimes see when walking in ancient forests. There were no pews, but only scattered cushions on which the nuns can sit or kneel. After letting the serenity of the chapel sink into us, we went outside to explore the grounds."

"On the far side of the chapel a cluster of people was gathered: the convent's nuns, a Franciscan priest, a small group of pilgrims, and, as I learned later, several workmen, including some loggers and two woodcarvers. We joined the pilgrims, who were all older women wearing similar plain outfits. They were all silently gazing at an arrangement of life-sized carved wooden figures. It was the most amazing work of religious art I have ever seen."

"The central figure was a female form, clothed in a flowing habit and caught up in an ecstatic pose. Her arms were uplifted and her own gaze was fixed on something high above her. The figure was suspended on fibrous ropes and held perhaps five feet off the ground. Gathered around her feet were four figures: on her left hand, a kneeling nun with a sheep and, on her right hand, a workman leaning on one knee and supported by a staff, his head bowed in humility, with a herding dog sitting next to him."

"The perfect silence of the sculptural array was matched by the rapt attention of the gathering. Then one of the nuns began to sing softly and the others joined her. The melody was haunting, ancient and beautiful; the words were in a language I didn't know, but they must have had profound meaning to the nuns, who sang in perfect unison with tears of joy running down their cheeks."

"After a long silence, the priest stepped forward, bowing to the community of nuns and welcoming us outsiders to this ceremony. He said we were honoring Mother Terra, who had brought a new spirituality to their motherhouse and a new life to the Poor Sisters who had settled there decades ago. Like their brother Francis, Terra had expanded the circle of love to embrace not only creatures of the wild but the forests themselves, with their glorious vegetation and the flowing waters and rich earth that sustained them. He lifted his face skyward and thanked Brother Sun for his life-giving rays and a billowing grey cloud for its generous rainfall. He ended his brief homily with a quiet prayer. Then he thanked the woodsmen for their skill and hard work in constructing these buildings, remembering the wider community of forest people whom they represented. Turning to the two men who were woodcarvers, he expressed the convent's gratitude for the exceptional creativity and skill their crew had shown in completing this magnificent sculptural tableaux. Later, we learned they had worked for over a month with a larger crew from a distant community of woodcarvers. These two had stayed behind to oversee the removal of the sculptures from the chapel and their temporary installation outdoors. As an after- thought, the priest thanked the trees of the forest for providing the wood needed to construct the buildings and the figures."

"When the ceremony was completed a nun welcomed us, along with the pilgrims, and offered to answer any questions we had. The pilgrims said they were oblates of The Poor Sisters and had come to see what their new spirituality of nature could mean for the religious order."

"My friend and I were deeply moved by the ceremony and the experience of the sacred sculptural tableaux. We lingered with the pilgrims, trying to gain a better understanding of what this new spirituality might be by overhearing the nun's modest responses to their questions. We gathered that most of the nuns had come to this site to create a new daughter convent because their motherhouse had recently grown too large for the life and work they were devoted to. The mother convent was about a two day journey down and back up into the eastern mountains. And that was the place that had been transformed by the nun they called 'Mother Terra.'"

"We needed to return to Mountain View before dark, especially since the western skies were darkening with rain clouds. My friend was speculating about how the monastic community might impact the local economy. He knew that the mother- house had become an important destination for pilgrims, not just Franciscans but other people interested in spiritual life. If that happened here in Mountain View there would need to be places to house and board visitors. I suggested that with this new tableaux it might be possible to have small replicas carved locally as mementoes, as well as books and other items related to the Franciscan way of life. The idea of having a small shop selling such religious artifacts excited my friend and, getting far ahead of what was already in place, we considered even wider markets for replicas of the tableaux."

The effects of the ample meal and the soothing heat of the fireplace were slowing the pace of the stout businessman. He concluded with a brief inventory of the merchandise he had contracted for, either to market back in the capital or to arrange for sale back in Mountain View. It was obvious how he relished all the negotiations these new transactions would require of him.

The keeper used this pause to bring a crystal decanter from the pantry. On a wooden tray were five delicate glasses, into which he poured generous portions of golden brandy. He explained how it was distilled from wine made using pears from the orchard of the monastery that provided the Inn's brandy. Then he passed the drinks to his guests, taking one for himself, and offered a toast to their health and safe travels.

It was the old priest's turn to speak. He had been getting increasingly agitated as the merchant spoke, and now began his narrative even before they had emptied their glasses.

"Well, this is quite extraordinary. I believe I can shed some light on how the Mountain View convent came to exist and what the origins of that dramatic sculptural array were. As I explained earlier, I have had an almost life-long fascination with St. Francis of Assisi. Even as a boy I was attracted to his way of practicing the virtues of humility, poverty and brotherly love—especially the way he saw our kinship with other creatures and the whole world of nature. But I was also a bookish boy and, so, was drawn to the world of learning. I suppose I could have become a scholarly monk or even a theologian, but the cloistered life didn't appeal to me. That's why I decided to become a parish priest and kept scholarly interests for my free time—as if a parish priest ever gets much of that."

"Over the years, I occasionally served the Church as a consultant regarding a wide array of Franciscan matters. As you may know, before Francis was made a saint he had a rather disruptive effect on the Church of his time. His ideals of poverty and service to the poor threatened many established religious communities. When his first followers resisted living an isolated cloistered life in favor of a mendicant life among the common people, that seemed like a condemnation of the conventional life of monks. But his teachings and practices were so obviously modelled after our Lord's way that they couldn't be directly challenged. And, almost from the beginning, he attracted so much support from commoners that it was unwise to simply reject him. Though Francis was indifferent to Church politics, ironically it was just such politics which swept him into early sainthood."

"Well, every settled institution or tradition resists change, especially if it comes suddenly and strikes deeply. So, the Church has been monitoring the Franciscans from the start, especially when important innovations arise. As long as the Franciscan religious work in out-of-the-way regions or keep themselves to isolated monasteries (yes, some of them have adopted a rather cloistered life), the Church remains fairly indifferent to them. But in recent years we have been hearing about new ideas and practices which may upset the established authority of the Church."

"That's where I come into the picture, and why I have spent the past week at the very motherhouse our businessman friend has just mentioned. 'Our Lady of the Mountains' is itself a young convent, established about twenty years ago. It was formed to create a home for nuns who want to lead a contemplative life in close proximity to wilderness and the remote settlements of simple people. As I learned firsthand, the nuns serve local farmers and woodsmen in various ways, while following a life of communal prayer and work. Some call this order 'The Poor Clares,' after their founder, one of the earliest female followers of Francis. Like her teacher, Clare adopted a life of extreme voluntary poverty and service to the poor and others who live on the fringes of society."

"At first the new convent seemed like a harmless haven for a few spiritual women. From the start they attracted the admiration and support of people living in the area. Naturally, the sisters offered basic education for the children there. But they also provided guidance on ways to improve care for their cows and goats, and ways to improve the fertility of their small fields and gardens. The men gladly provided stout logs for the small church and adjoining cloister. They used their large oxen to move timbers to the building site and then raise them to create the high walls. The chapel also served as the church for local people."

"When I first arrived at the convent I was amazed by the beauty of their church, so primitive and yet so holy. The roof is pitched sharply to shed deep snow and the windows are tall and narrow, with shutters to keep out bad weather. The appearance is very like that of the Mountain View chapel our friend just described."

"After I introduced myself, the Mother Superior led me around the little church and its grounds. As we walked slowly, pausing at various points of special interest, this quiet holy woman made clear to me why she and a small band of sisters had the courage to leave their own motherhouse and seek such a wild isolated place to establish a new community. The Mother Superior had a vision of a way to live in deeper intimacy with the untamed natural world, which she felt had to be set apart from the world ruled by merely human ideas and purposes. As far as possible, her small group wanted to live directly from the earth: drink and bathe in cold mountain streams, eat what the forest and open fields gave them as simple gatherers and gardeners, build humble shelters from unsawn timber, use only fallen deadwood for their fires, and so on."

"Almost from their first days high in these mountains they encountered small settlements of hearty pioneers who already had worked out much of what is necessary for any such way of living. Without the help and support of those forest dwellers the convent might never have survived the first harsh winter. In addition to providing food and firewood, their neighbors did much of the difficult manual labor required to build a humble cloister, adjacent to a small chapel. Both were constructed of round logs cut on site and chinked with moss and heavy clay."

"Each following year the bonds between native foresters and the spiritual community deepened, with some of the younger forest women joining the community. The people were drawn to the convent's distinctive forms of worship, which blended traditional Christian rites with liturgies tied to the natural cycles of their mountainous location. Some of the forest people joined them in solstice ceremonies in deep winter and late spring, often outdoors in their contemplative garden and always revealing powerful connections between Christian understanding and the mysteries of nature."

"The story of the garden was fascinating. About a year after Sister Terra arrived, a young man came to the convent offering to be their handyman, doing whatever work that needed to be done. From the start it was evident that the man had not only many useful talents but also a strong spiritual inclination. He always joined the nuns in their worship, staying at the fringe of the community but engaging fully in their worship. It was this man who began the garden project."

"One day he asked to speak with the Mother Superior and Sister Terra about a vision he had in a dream. In it he saw a stream of mountain water emerging from beside the chapel. Around it was built a small grotto that echoed the bubbling water. He saw the stream finding a winding path away from the chapel amid boulders before spilling down the plateau to the farmers' little fields below. There was a low stone wall enclosing the garden, creating a world that both imitated the surrounding mountain woods and intensified its presence. Various shrubs and small trees mixed with mossy boulders and seasonal flowers and berries, which added color. It would be a way for the sisters to sometimes worship outdoors but without needing to trek into the encompassing forest."

"The Mother and Sister Terra saw the man's passion and the potential of such a spiritual garden. They encouraged him to search for the hidden spring. Just one day's digging exposed a strong flow of pure water that worked through the rocks underground but was close enough to the surface to gush out once a path was opened for it. This was, in fact, the source of an artesian spring that flowed out further down the mountain and eventually fed Crazy Creek."

"In the following year the caretaker enlisted men from the forest community to help locate and site an assortment of large boulders along the winding course of the stream. Without the use of their massive oxen the task would have been impossible. They also used stone-boats to haul slabs of rock to build a grotto and a low stacked-stone wall to enclose the garden. The nuns searched in the surrounding forest for shrubs, small evergreen trees, ferns and other native vegetation to create a remarkably natural forest-like setting. The grotto was the centerpiece of the garden, with flat boulders arrayed in front of it where the nuns and others could recline during their ceremonies."

"The caretaker was granted permission to build a small hut in a corner of the garden so he was easily available to the convent to serve its needs and oversee the care of the garden. His given name was Maurice and soon all the nuns called him 'Brother Maurice.' The Brother was a quiet presence at all the services in the liturgical day so, when he didn't appear one morning for the predawn assembly' a sister went to check on him. She found him curled on his mat, seemingly asleep but actually deceased."

"The loss of Brother Maurice shocked the community. He had seemed so young and strong, so reliable in his work. It was suddenly clear how much his labors and imagination enriched the life of the convent. The nuns honored their brother with a commemorative service and his burial in the garden beside his hut."

"To conclude her story of Brother Maurice, the Mother Superior took me to a small display in a corner of the chapel, concealed by a simple screen. On a shelf was an array of Maurice's hand tools, the leather vest he always wore, and a slender wooden object that was found in an inner pocket of the vest when his body was prepared for burial."

"It is that wooden case and its contents which will most astonish you. I have been eager to tell you about it since our business friend first described the religious tableaux he admired at the Mountain View convent. For, when the Mother showed me the wooden object, I first realized that the small 6"x 8" wooden object was actually a slender container. It was made of a dark fine-grained wood, I think walnut, with rounded corners and edges. The surface was smooth and glowed from being in contact with its leather pocket for so long. Although it appeared to be solid, a simple twist by Mother's hands and the two halves of the object fell open. Inside was a delicate tiny version of the very tableaux we have just heard described: a female figure suspended above two kneeling humans and their accompanying animals. The figures were carved in a golden wood and nestled in matching niches to secure them. Although the figures were diminutive, each was carved in amazing detail. The Mother told me that she could clearly recognize even the facial features of Sister Terra in the elevated figure and the distinctive aspects of Brother Maurice's handsome face in the kneeling pilgrim."

"Well, I have already assumed your patience too long, but I had to provide some setting for this remarkable story, which sheds so much light on what has happened at the Mountain View convent. As the Mother Superior explained, that community is a daughter colony of Our Lady of the Mountains. Its nuns had all been deeply affected by the wilderness spirituality of Sister Terra, so when the need to create a daughter convent arose, these sisters eagerly offered to be the pioneers for a new community. From the start, they began referring to Sister Terra as 'Mother' and modelled their liturgies and life ever closer to Terra's example. That's what inspired the idea of the tableaux which Brother Maurice's devotional wooden case had first revealed."

"I dearly wanted to meet Sister Terra, but she was off in the wilderness for one of her regular solitary retreats. The Mother Superior said that Terra always followed the promptings of nature and the divine spirit, so she couldn't be expected to go by a schedule. Still, I lingered a couple extra days, offering my priestly services to this isolated community. Then I started my journey home."

With that, the priest concluded. The inn keeper suggested that they all stand up and walk around the sitting area a while to stretch their legs and give themselves time to ponder the surprising coincidence of the two stories they had just heard. But soon the shop-keeper was eager to have his turn, promising that the coincidences were going to continue.

"Well, as you will see shortly, my own recent travels have also added a chapter to the story which is unfolding for us this evening. As I said earlier, I maintain a small shop near the capital which features books on local crafts and history and a nice sampling of the artifacts and artwork produced in this region. For many years it has been my practice in the off-seasons to travel about to discover solitary artisans or small guild settlements. That adds new items for my shop and expands my notebooks on these fascinating craftsmen. My friends frequently urge me to bring my knowledge and observations to some conclusion by writing a book on these subjects."

"That is why I have spent my recent days in the small settlement of Saint Francis. It is home to several guilds of traditional woodworkers and carvers who chose their site generations ago because of the variety of hardwoods growing at that elevation. It is a community of over a hundred, including the guild members' families and an array of others whose work supports them. So, there are farmers, carpenters, bakers, small merchants, and such. The place is called 'Saint Francis' and has a little church with one priest."

"The main source of outside income comes from the work of the guildsmen. They specialize in creating wood products for churches and religious communities. While I visited Saint Francis I was able to tour all of their shops: some featured pews and other simple church furnishings; others specialized in pulpits, lecterns and baptismals. Perhaps most striking of all were the elaborate altars designed and produced in a larger shop. Almost all of their work was commissioned by congregations and spiritual communities who sent envoys to Saint Francis to transform their generic ideas into precise designs and, then, into finished fine wood results. The community had its own woodsmen and stream-powered sawmill to provide the raw materials for its creations."

"What especially struck me was the range of woodworking skills needed to create such items. Even a simple pew was a combination of plank seats curved for comfort, strong end-pieces that had to harmonize with items in the altar area, and often intricate small carved features. One shop produced only carved plaques or sculptures of the stations of the cross. Another focused on images of St. Francis and related figures. Yet another created wooden chalices, cups and platters for the Eucharist."

"While I was admiring a particularly striking tableaux of St. Francis and attendant animals, the master of the shop began telling me about the young apprentice who had created it years before. He said the young man often did uncommissioned items in his free time, perfecting his skill in miniature carving while also deepening his personal devotion to the Saint. Responding to my interest, he brought out several more examples of the young man's work. What especially struck me was the precision of each figure and the sense of their living presence in each arrangement."

"I asked whether I could meet this carver to learn more about his artistry, but the master told me the youth had left the community years ago. He had travelled west on the narrow path that winds along the mountain front, bound for a small Franciscan convent. I expressed surprise that he would go to a convent rather than a monastery if he was seeking a religious life. That led the master to tell me about what was really motivating the apprentice carver."

"He had fallen in love with a young woman in Saint Francis. Not just any local girl, but the youngest daughter of the richest man in the community. This man's family had been the founders of the village's oldest guild and were instrumental in moving it to this remote mountain setting. Because he was the patriarch of the extended family which had masters in many of the shops, this man had wealth and influence far beyond anyone else in Saint Francis."

"But, surprisingly, his youngest and dearest child had shown no interest in the privileges that would naturally come to her. While her sisters studied with a private tutor, she insisted on going to the one-room school for village children. Even as a child she loved to walk out among the villagers and their shops and homes. She showed an exceptional compassion for anyone who was sick, injured or otherwise disabled. And her compassion extended to the animals of the community. She would carry a bag with scraps from her family's kitchen and share them with dogs, sheep, chickens, and other creatures she met. Often, she would have a small band of begging creatures following her. If a dog was scrawny or favored an injured leg, she would find its owner and offer to help with its care. When a cat had a litter too large for its owner to care for, the girl would contrive to have mother and kits brought to her home. Her parents, especially her father, chastised the girl and explained her proper place in the village, but she just smiled sweetly and continued her ways."

"Like everyone else in the little village, the young carver knew about this girl and her unusual ways. He often talked about her with his fellow workers: perhaps she was just taking the tales of St. Francis to extremes and too literally; perhaps she felt guilty about her family's wealth and was trying to apologize for it; perhaps it was just some passing form of childish rebellion. But the young apprentice said he was sure it was some deeper spiritual calling. In fact, when he asked the priest about it the Father said he had noticed the girl's spirit of humility and compassion for all living things long before she could have learned any tales about Francis. There was an almost innate spiritual longing in her."

"As the girl approached womanhood, her father was distressed by her lack of interest in the normal things her older sisters had so eagerly embraced: wearing fashionable clothes, reading romantic literature, dreaming about some appropriate young man (probably not from their village), and so on. When she began going off into the surrounding wilderness alone and returning home in a kind of dazed ecstasy he became alarmed."

"As the carver learned later from their priest, the girl came to him to get a better sense of the life and teachings of St. Francis. When she learned about a convent of Franciscan sisters just two days west along the mountain front, she immediately made plans to go there. She said a tearful farewell to her family, put a few essentials in a backpack, and set off on her journey."

"The shop master recalled how the girl's departure stunned his best apprentice. He moped around the shop, worrying out loud about her safety and her likely regrets about deserting her family. The master saw the young man laboring intently over small figures he carved from various woods; though he never was able to examine them closely, he was sure they were figures of the girl."

"Over the following year the carver grew evermore withdrawn and pensive. Then one day after their work was done he lingered to talk with the master. He had lost his zest for carving and wanted to follow a simpler more spiritual path. After settling a few personal matters, he too strapped on a backpack and began his walk across the face of the mountains."

"Of course, I learned a great deal more about this village of craftsmen. I even obtained an assortment of small pieces (carvings and models) to take home to my shop. Understandably, the master wouldn't part with any of the figures left by the apprentice. How I wish I had some now to show you his exquisite work. For nothing struck me as powerfully as this story of a young man I never met. Like our priest friend, my most compelling encounter was with a person I never met, but whose spirit and impacts gave our places of visitation their most vivid meaning."

Again, a speaker's story was followed by a moment of deep silence. Only the gentle sounds of the dying fire and the song of a solitary mournful cricket somewhere in the room served as background to each man's separate musings.

The young man broke the silence, asking the inn keeper if they might enjoy another glass of his honey-sweet brandy. Then he offered a toast: "Here's to this wonderful evening, which has brought us so mysteriously together from our separate paths and given us such an improbable course of stories. May we always remember and ponder these things." Then he began his own reflections.

"Unlike you gentlemen, I as yet have no tale to tell of my journey, since I am just setting out on it. But now I have an itinerary and a purpose. And, as if this was all pre-arranged, the stories you have shared fit perfectly into the geography of my own mind. As I explained during dinner, I have recently completed my dissertation on the ways in which deep currents of culture arise from charismatic individuals. People whose presence far exceeds their humble origins, who seem to be encompassed in auras and emanations and whose lives are accompanied by signs and wonders. We meet such individuals in folktales and myths, at the fountainhead of philosophy and religion, art and inventive genius. And often these individuals seem perplexed themselves about how they became vessels chosen to carry such precious benefices."

"Thus, as I listened to your stories unfolding, I somewhat understood how the nuns' adoration of Sister Terra could lead them to transform a wild mountain place into a spiritual community; how the actual Terra could be transfigured into a divine mother and lifted up as an object of devotion. But who was the actual sister and where did this powerful sculptural tableaux come from? We might think that the garden tableaux at Mountain View was simply an expanded version of the gardener's hidden miniatures, and that the brother's creation was inspired by his adoration of the girl. So, it all goes back to his idealizing of a simple romantic love. But why was her spirituality so attractive to him, so that instead of courting her he adored her? And what were the origins of the girl's deep love of all creatures and of the wilderness itself?"

"I don't have good answers, yet, but I can see clues from many myths and traditional tales. Our learned Father has already told us a little about how Francis' compassion ignited many hearts with love for the lowly and for nature's creatures, with a new sense of kinship that broke open the hard shells that usually restrict our capacity to care. But, of course, Francis himself was likewise transformed by the example and teachings of our Lord. And when we search for Jesus' abundant love we are driven back to tales of his divine origins. It seems that sometimes people are like dry tinder and that a single spark of inspiration can ignite them and produce fires that expand indefinitely. Often the fires burn down, leaving only grey ashes and lingering warmth. But if a few embers lie hidden under that cover, just a small breath of air can ignite a new blaze, if only the proper tinder is at hand."

"Well, that's getting rather metaphorical, but I am trying to grasp how it is that single individuals or small bands of followers can transform the world. These stories you have shared are themselves an inspiration to my inquiring mind. You have given me an itinerary. First, I will ride to Saint Francis to retrace some of the shopkeeper's steps and see firsthand where the tale of the maiden and the carver began. Then I will take their path along the front of the mountains to Our Lady of the Mountains to experience the contemplative garden and the carver's personal tableaux. It is my fondest hope to behold Sister Terra herself. Finally, I will continue to the convent at Mountain View to join the nuns in worship and meditate in their garden, with its sublime tableaux. By such means I hope to better understand how the first impulses of Terra's love continue to change the world."

The Inn keeper broke the silence by stirring the ashes in the fireplace, exposing a few glowing coals he could use to rekindle a fire that would hold through the chilly night. The guests watched this wordless process, each pondering the young man's metaphor as they gradually shifted to the thought of a good sleep. The keeper bade them a "Good Night" and promised a substantial breakfast before they set out on the next stages of their travels.

III - The Dwarf

I - Origins

He did not understand how he had become what he was, though he knew enough to know it was by some uncommon means. Even he realized he was grotesque, if measured by the common standards of humankind. Something was deeply contorted in him, in his outward appearance and his inward nature. Perhaps it was some curse or an anomaly of nature that had shaped him so. Perhaps his parents or creator had dabbled in forbidden things or made some terrible mistake. But why should he suffer for the deficiencies of others? Better to be an accident of nature, like a misshapen oak burl or a two-headed calf: then there would be no one to blame, any more than one would curse the lightning which strikes a young tree and leaves it disfigured and weak, but still alive.

He must be some sort of man, only solitary and odd. He had realized that when he saw the humans toiling in their fields or walking in their village streets; for they had limbs and upright posture and a lifted head as he did. Perhaps he was some unnatural mixed creature, like a centaur or mermaid. He certainly was intrigued by what it would be like to be some other sort of being—like a wild beast, but with enough of his own mind to realize his original nature.

When he watched a trout holding itself in the shelter of a river boulder, waiting for a mayfly to drift overhead, he could try to imagine its intense concentration and its sudden explosion to the surface to seize the insect. When spring brought jubilant songs from the throat of a courting cardinal, he felt its longing and its latent talent for building a proper nest. But neither the fish nor the bird could have the double consciousness the dwarf desired. They were simply what they were.

Only later in life would he recall sacrificing his simple human nature to gain the powers needed to make such transformations. His mixed nature was due neither to another's curse or mistake nor to a mere accident. It was a necessary consequence of his own choosing. But why?

As far back as he could recall he had lived a solitary life, an odd kind of hermit dwelling in a vast virgin forest. He lived completely on what the forest world provided him for food, shelter and companionship. And yet, from early on, he realized he had no real kin, no common kind. Somehow, he had acquired a language sufficient for his inner musings and his conversations with the natural world. But he had no true companion with whom to share his inner life.

II - The Maiden

In a broad grassland clearing near the border of the same forest there was a solitary castle, the sheltered dwelling of a lord and his lady, with a beloved daughter just nearing womanhood. The princess was an only child and, so, the single object of her parents' hopes and doting. Though their castle was secure in its isolation, and modestly luxurious in its accommodations, it was a lonely place for the girl to grow up. Early on she had tired of dolls and toy animals. Stories of fanciful creatures and distant worlds intrigued her young mind, but she preferred the wilderness world surrounding the castle. So, she often hiked in the encircling prairie, accompanied by her large shaggy dog. When weather permitted and her spirit wanted adventure and mystery, she would take a horse and explore the vast forest beyond the broad clearing which encompassed their home.

Occasionally there were guests in the castle, providing the princess with a small circle of friends. But when her friends left, she was utterly cut off from them. That's how she got the desire to have messenger pigeons. Her parents arranged for her to have six pigeons, along with a trainer who taught the pure white birds to follow two courses between the castle and a pair of villages where her friends lived beyond the forest.

III - Transformations

One day, the dwarf saw a red-tailed hawk perched high in a bare lightning-struck oak. Its position provided a sweeping view of the forest floor, which it surveyed with intense attention. The dwarf was trying to imagine what the raptor was experiencing as it tilted its alert head and swiveled it from side to side. Perhaps a mole tunneling under the fallen leaves, or a busy squirrel foraging for fallen hickory nuts. Suddenly, he realized he wasn't merely imagining what the hawk was scanning — that was also his experience. He even felt the beating heart of the bird and the tensing of the muscles in his wings. And then he plunged down like a spear, crashing into a mound of leaves and seizing a small dark squirming body in his locked talons. His powerful wings spread and flapped immediately, lifting him into the radiant air and returning him to his high perch. The dwarf had fed almost solely on plants and their fruit and seeds. But now he felt the ferocity of the hawk's feeding as his sharp beak tore the mole open and ripped out its viscera. The tiny rodent was pinned against a thick branch as it was dismembered and consumed.

When the hawk finished it remained on its bare perch, drowsing in the warm sunlight. The dwarf also settled into a contented torpor. As the great bird began to stir and stretch its wings, the dwarf awakened to find himself separate and curled on the ground again. He gazed up in wonder at the majestic raptor. Such creatures rarely came into the forest, preferring open fields and the edges of the forest where rodents were more common and easier to see and hunt. Only in the transitional times of early spring and late autumn did they extend their range into the forest. Winter would drive most rodents into their dens for hibernation.

The dwarf wanted to follow the hawk back to its familiar hunting grounds, so, when the bird lifted from the top of the tree and turned west, the dwarf scrambled after it. But his short legs were no match for those sweeping wings, so he was soon left behind, panting and stumbling through the undergrowth. When he fell, exhausted, he felt himself being lifted, and then he was united with the hawk again, winging farther west with each deep stroke of those wings.

Vast bare forest stretched before him, until a broad clearing came into view. The hawk banked north and began a wide slow circling of what at first seemed to be a massive stone mound set in the middle of the opening. When the hawk drew closer, the dwarf could see a small castle on top of the rocky base, like an island in a sea of prairie. Circling down, the hawk tilted its head and the dwarf saw a human figure standing amid specks of white. Closer still, he saw that it was a young woman feeding a small flock of pigeons.

Just as the dwarf started pondering what this scene meant, the shadow of the hawk swept across the rooftop, startling the pigeons and causing the woman to look up. The dwarf was struck by her beauty but saw her alarm and wished that the hawk had not startled her, though he was so glad to have had this brief vision. Then the hawk curved away and rose higher, lifting its gaze to the horizon as it continued its flight west.

When the hawk finally settled in a tree top near the outer limits of the forest, the dwarf realized he was far from his home. He imagined being back in the narrow ravine that had sheltered him for so long, with his small dark cave seeming like a haven for his restless spirit. Then he found himself back there, lying on a bed of dry rushes and leaves. But his mind was whirling with images from his winged adventure — and the vision of the woman would not let him sleep.

IV - Encounter

One spring day, when the greening world was jubilant with bird song and the air fresh with the scent of new life, the princess went to the stables and asked the stable hand to saddle her young stallion. Her father had encouraged her to learn the arts of riding and, hopefully, hunting from horseback. She had become accomplished with the bow, but only when drawing it back to release her arrows at stationary inanimate targets. And only with both feet set firmly on level ground, with no hurry to loose her arrows. This morning, the master of the castle suggested that the day was perfect for his daughter to ride afield with her archery gear over her shoulder.

It was the season of renewal and she might encounter deer so preoccupied with new browse that she could approach them unnoticed. There was no thought of actual hunting, but learning how to approach game animals and practice drawing her bow astride her stallion would give her invaluable lessons for becoming a real huntress. So, with the stable hand riding beside her, the princess rode out into the greening meadows, delighting in the flight and songs of the returning birds.

The princess indulged her father's wishes, but with no intention of adopting the mind of a hunter, much less actually taking aim at any game. It was a glorious morning and she did love to ride across the wide meadow and into the forest. When they were beyond the range of what she could view from the castle ramparts she could see the edge of the forest. Some trees were already crowned with swelling buds, even some flowering redbuds and dogwoods. The woods were alive with the mating calls and passionate chasing of returning birds. When she approached boggy areas, the air scintillated with the sounds of tree frogs announcing their emergence from winter's sleep. The sense of wakening exuberant life was intoxicating.

From time to time, the stable hand would stop them so he could ride ahead to set up targets for the princess. He used heaps of brush or long grass to simulate browsing deer or feeding turkeys, finding places where she would come upon them unexpectedly. Then she would have to learn how to approach silently and slowly, attentive to the wind so their scent would not alarm the quarry. Soon, the princess was enjoying this hunting exercise like playing a game. As they moved along the wooded edges, she was alert to every bend or sheltering grove. And, when she spied a brushy 'deer' or a grass-formed 'goose,' she would raise her hand to stop her companion and ponder the best approach. Then she would remove the bow from her shoulder, take an arrow from its quiver, notch it to the taut string, and draw back before releasing it. When the arrow found its mark, she wanted to shout, but caught herself—she didn't want to startle other game nearby.

But when the stable hand retrieved her arrows, she was already breathing slower and thinking about real encounters. She imagined actual creatures lying dead before her and her arrow heads coated with their innocent blood. No, she didn't ever want to be a real hunter. Then, with her mind still fixed on the dreadful thought of killing a wild creature, the princess saw something moving in a grove of small willow trees. The arched branches were already thick with new leaves so, at first, she couldn't make out what was shaking them. Suddenly she realized that what she had taken as bare dark branches was actually the massive rack of a stag's antlers, not yet shed. She was shaken by the presence of such a large powerful creature and surprisingly glad she had her bow and the skill to use it.

But, when the beast lifted its head and stepped into the open, her mounting fear was overcome by the beauty of the stag's majestic presence. He tipped his head back, sniffing the air, and shook his rack as if to display his dangerous power to whatever was disturbing his browse. For a moment, the princess and the stag considered each other, both threatened and fascinated. Then the black stallion, tense and apprehensive, whinnied. The stag slowly turned away and disappeared beyond the willow grove.

The princess remained astride her mount, unmoving but deeply moved. When her eyes were joined with the creature's steady gaze, she had felt something stir in her. He was so wild and alien, but his proud stance and unwavering gaze showed his nobility.

V - Return to the Castle

In truth, the dwarf was incarnated in the majestic stag. He had encountered the animal earlier that morning. No other forest creature was as large and forbidding; so, when the dwarf first saw this stag feeding on tender new twigs and fresh grasses, he shivered with fear. What if the stag sensed him and charged, running him down and piercing him with those daggers? But, when the beast turned and saw the small creature huddling under a bush, the dwarf felt the stag's strength and fearlessness. Immediately, he was transported into the animal's psyche, shaking his broad rack and returning to his feeding.

As they moved out onto the grassy meadow, the dwarf felt the full sunlight warm his furry back. Prairie birds were filling the air with unfamiliar songs—larks of different kinds, bobolinks and bluebirds joined in a joyous chorus. The dwarf began to yearn to be one of them, to search for insects among the grasses, to raise his courting song in hope of a response, to chase the mate he had already found.

But the stag had moved west over a low ridge and had stopped to consider a dark rocky pyramid in the distance. Thr dwarf realized that it was the castle he had once seen through a hawk's keen eyes. It was where she lived, the princess in white. His heart leaped and he longed to see her.

Then he was on the castle rooftop, eagerly awaiting the opening of the large cage he shared with five other white pigeons. He saw the young woman approaching with a small bucket. He felt the excitement of the other birds and knew it as his own. She was coming to feed her winged messengers. As soon as the cage door was opened the little flock rushed out, swirling around the princess before they all alighted on the edges of the cage.

She was talking to them, her voice soft and musical. She poured several heaps of seed onto trays atop the cage, shushing the clamoring creatures and gently separating them so they could all share the food. "There, there, dear friends. No need to crowd each other. There's plenty for each of you. Go slowly, it's such a glorious day. Later one of you must carry greetings to my friend in Ravenwood. But first I want to let you free to fly around the castle and its fields."

Then she made a broad sweep with her right hand and the little flock sprang into the air and began circling overhead. The dwarf went with them as if he knew this free flight from long experience. They swooped and circled the castle, the dwarf keeping his yellow eyes fixed on the maiden. When they dropped back down to the rooftop and settled near the cage, one pigeon landed beside the princess. It was the dwarf-bearing pigeon, cooing and fluffing itself for her attention. The princess took a small handful of grain and offered it to the bird. It was a simple offering, but the dwarf almost swooned as the bird gently pecked at the maiden's open palm.

Soon, the maiden's dog came bounding to the rooftop, wagging its tail and trying to get the girl to follow it back into the castle. She called the pigeons to their cage and closed the door behind them. Then she said goodnight to the little flock and followed the attentive dog down the stairs. As the dwarf began to settle into his pigeon rest, he realized that he had returned to his distant cave and was sinking into a deep sleep.

After that, the dwarf's mind was alive with thoughts of the princess. Waking and dreaming, he found himself imagining her. Since he had never been inside a castle and knew nothing about that interior life, he could hardly envision any details of her hidden life. Still, he tried to picture the princess taking her meals, reading fine books and perhaps playing music or composing letters for her friends. Then he thought of her dog: how fortunate he was to be close to her as she moved about the castle. He could be her companion throughout the day, close enough to receive her gentle petting and words of affection. Perhaps he could even sleep beside her, warming her on wintry nights

Then, lost in such envious daydreams, the dwarf wakened to find himself embodied in the golden dog. He was lying on a rug beside the princess as she played upon a small harp. It was some simple folk melody, with delicate passages that flowed from her fingers as they plucked the strings. When her sweet voice joined the harp's gentle voice, the dog tilted his head attentively and the dwarf was caught up in the romantic lyrics. It was an old ballad about a maiden longing for her absent lover, who was off on some dangerous mission. The dwarf was entranced and, when the dog sighed quietly, it was his sigh as well. At the conclusion of the song, the princess reached down and rubbed the dog behind his floppy ears, telling him what a good friend he was.

VI - The Rose Bush

After that transformation, the dwarf often shuttled back and forth between his secret cave and its environs (whenever the dog slept or was separated from the princess) and the castle and its grounds (when he accompanied her). One morning, when the princess was walking in one of the castle's gardens, she paused to inspect a rose bush, trimmed to make a perfect sphere. The tips of the delicate branches were festooned with buds just starting to press out of the tight green sleeves which clasped the waking scarlet flowers.

When the princess began speaking to the bush, the dog heard and the dwarf understood her hushed words. "I know it's still too soon for your flowering, dear bush; but I have longed to see your beautiful blossoms and smell your rich fragrances so often through our long winter. How eagerly I await your unfolding."

Suddenly, the dwarf felt a strange transfiguration and then he was incarnate in the rose bush. He could no longer hear or comprehend the words coming from the lips of the princess, but he felt a surge of life swell up from his roots and flow through his branches and stems until it slowly pressed the buds open. The princess was startled and mystified by this florid eruption, but she knew it was some kind of miracle. It was as if nature was offering her a gift: not in the usual way that it graced her days, but in this extraordinary revelation.

The princess leaned close to the sphere of blood-red flowers and inhaled deeply, filling her lungs and swirling mind with the rich fragrance. She stayed close to the wondrous bush for a long time, gently touching the trembling blossoms and thanking the bush for its unseasonal gift. Then she slid her fingers beneath an especially lush blossom and plucked it from its stem. She pressed the fleshy petals against her face, kissing them and drinking their spicy perfume with her inhalations. When she inserted the flower in the dark hair behind her ear the dwarf rejoined the dog and followed his beloved friend back inside the castle.

Later, back in his dark cave, the dwarf pondered what had happened to him. He had gradually lost his fascination with natural creatures and become absorbed in a human world. It was as if, now, all his incarnations took him from his secluded natural realm to the castle, with its pigeons, dog and gardens. And all of that was due to the attraction of the princess—the human who was luring him out of his feral world.

But for all his closeness, even intimacy, with the princess, he was still completely hidden from her in his human form. That was fortunate, since he remained a disfigured and alien creature that would shock and offend any human being. So, the dwarf despaired of ever knowing the fulness of his love and being able to manifest it to the beloved princess.

Then, a totally unimagined transformation liberated the dwarf from his seemingly hopeless quandary. He was back at the castle, embodied in the faithful dog as it followed the princess to the stables. It was near the close of springtime, when the pale new leaves were reaching their fulness and growing dark with the deep greens of summer.

The stable hand saw the princess walking to the stable as he worked in her flower garden. He left his tools and hurried to reach the corral ahead of the lady. To understand his haste, you must know some of the young man's story.

VII - The Stable Hand

The stable hand was not an ordinary servant. In fact, he was the only son of a prominent family in the village of Ravenwood, raised to someday take his father's place as a wealthy land owner and business man. But his tutors and wide reading had opened his mind to more romantic possibilities. Perhaps he could join an expedition to some remote region to study its exotic flora and fauna, its unimaginable wilderness. Or he might travel in some unknown kingdom and find a beautiful princess and become her troubadour and champion.

So, as he approached maturity, he asked his father for a year of wandering education. The father was puzzled and apprehensive about his son's request; but he knew that educated youths sometimes took a year of wandering abroad to round out their formal bookish schooling. Besides, he didn't want to stifle his bright son and create an unnecessary divide between them. So, when the day of departure arrived, the young man strapped on his backpack, said farewell to his parents, and set off on his seemingly indefinite journey.

But the youth already had his immediate destination in mind, and it wasn't as far off and uncertain as his worrying parents imagined. He had learned about an intriguing place from a close friend. She was a girl of his age whose parents had sometimes visited a family who lived in a remote castle in the midst of the Great Forest. That family had a beautiful young daughter who was exceptionally sheltered from the world. She kept messenger pigeons so she could correspond with her few friends. He knew he had to begin his quest by going there.

When he learned from his friend that the head servant of the castle was seeking an apprentice to train as his replacement when he retired, the youth got a startling idea. He could arrive at the castle presenting himself as a simple peasant youth seeking work and training. That would allow him to experience first-hand what it must be like to belong to the world of commoners.

Although he had befriended a couple of his own family's male servants, he was never sure how much they were simply indulging his curiosity while concealing their suspicions and differences from him. His own suspicions extended to many of the young women with whom his parents encircled him, hoping he would find a suitable match. How much of their affectionate attention was genuine and how much was calculated to ensnare him? He wanted others to know him as he was in himself, not as the only son of his wealthy family.

So, as soon as he left his parents, he replaced his fine clothing with the humble garb of a peasant lad and set out on foot in search of the castle. As he got closer to the Great Forest, the dirt road gave way to a little-used trail, with small isolated farms and the simple dwellings of people who lived by foraging and hunting. The people were at first distrustful, but helped him when he explained his destination.

What they told him of the castle fired his expectations. The family of the castle were kind and generous masters who, for all their wealth, chose to live a modest secluded life. They had a circle of servants who tended the gardens and small farm that supplied most of the food needed: some sheep and goats, poultry, draft horses and a few for drawing a carriage and riding. Farm hands also provided firewood from the nearby forest and planted and harvested wheat and other crops. In addition, they hunted and fished to supply the kitchen. The young man learned that most of the servants were people who had grown up in the pioneering families that he had encountered.

When he entered the outer reaches of the forest, he realized more clearly how isolated and self-sufficient the world of the castle must be. The narrow trail often felt like a green tunnel under the massive overarching trees. Finally, as the trees began to open into small clearings, he knew he was getting close to his destination. Soon, he was out in broad rolling grassland, like a vast pale-green lake: in the distance, he saw a dark island—the castle.

As he drew near, he could see the large stone structure encircled with farm buildings and the servants' cottages. The gardens and orchard were in good order and seemed to be flourishing. Surely there was work there that he could do.

Before he reached the gate of the farming compound, a large golden dog walked out to greet him with a deep loud bark. Behind him came an elderly man who introduced himself as the overseer of the farm. The youth's rustic appearance matched the vague account he gave of his origins and intentions. Yes, there was work for him and opportunities for learning farming skills. The overseer told how his old age was reducing his ability to do hard labor in the barns and gardens, especially since he had to manage the work of the other servants. Perhaps, if the youth showed promise, he might become the overseer's assistant. He would confer with the master about hiring a new hand.

When the master met the young man, he was surprised by his manners and soft hands: not what he was expecting from a peasant seeking work. But the youth seemed intelligent and earnest, especially important as someone who might one day succeed the overseer. So, he was provided a small space in the stable loft and a place was set for him at the servants' table.

Soon, he was settled into the world of the outdoor servants. Right away, his riding skills and love of gardening were being used as he fit into whatever work was needed. Though the youth was often silent and always soft spoken, the overseer saw that he was a trustworthy and competent servant. The lord of the castle was given good reports of the young man and his work. After a short time, the master was happy to have someone to entrust with his daughter when she wanted to ride afield and learn the skills suited to her life in this wilderness domain.

Thus, the youthful servant became the instructor and companion of the princess, their youth and enjoyment of the surrounding natural world drawing them into an unexpected friendship. She shared her intimate knowledge of the environment surrounding the castle and was surprised that someone else could be so attuned to.

VIII - Final Union

The maiden and her dog reached the stable just as the young servant also arrived. There was an immediate excitement in their conversation as the maiden assisted in saddling their horses and explained why she wanted to get an early start. She wanted to experience the quiet wakening of a small marsh at the edge of the forest. The dwarf was feeling left out of her plans as the pair mounted up. Then the maiden noticed the sulking dog and apologized to him, explaining why he had to stay behind. He followed them as they passed through a gate opening onto the prairie, stopping as his longing gaze went with them. He listened to the girl's happy voice until it became almost inaudible.

But then, in a blink, the dwarf felt like the princess was talking directly to him in her gentle way. He was riding close beside her, feeling the young stallion moving under him as he held its reins. Somehow, his longing to join the princess had transported the dwarf into the young man and he felt the servant's mind and heart as his own. He was captivated by the maiden's enthusiasm and easy acceptance of a mere servant as a friend. Suddenly, the stable hand became more talkative, asking about various plants and creatures they encountered.

When they reached the wetlands, they dismounted and walked along the boggy edges of a small pond. Frogs were croaking in the dense rushes, then going silent amid the wet plops they made trying to get away. A great blue heron came swooping down and landed nearby, immediately striking a hunting pose as he tilted his head in search of the scrambling frogs. Responding to the young man's questions, the princess explained some of the circle of life and death in this solitary watery world.

Then she pointed out the beaver lodges rising from the pond like the shelters of woodland people. The dwarf attended to every word and, with the equally attentive mind of the servant, was fascinated with her rich knowledge of these mysterious creatures. It was as if, somehow, she had access to what the beaver experienced and how their distinctive hidden world worked.

It seemed to the dwarf that, if he tried to enter the world of the beaver, he could know such things directly rather than by patient observation and imaginings. But, for now, he preferred to be with the young man, learning from their lovely teacher.

The morning passed seamlessly, with the double mind of the servant-dwarf an eager recipient of the maiden's tutelage as they explored the forest world. The maiden's words came to them as the spontaneous sharing of her deep understanding of what they experienced, rather than like a lesson for novices.

As the mounting sun began to blend everything into a common light and the early chill faded into a dulling warmth, the entranced riders turned their horses homeward. But as the castle came into view, each one sensed a profound new union—though only the dwarf knew it was threefold.

IX - A Three-fold Love

Even before the stable hand had seen and then met the daughter, he had gathered from the servants that she was something of a free spirit, often riding out alone to the surrounding meadows and deep forests to enjoy the world of nature beyond human alterations. And the servants frequently spoke of her openness and generosity with them. When she came outside, she always insisted on helping with stable chores or working in the gardens. Her enjoyment and eagerness were genuine, without a trace of superiority. In fact, like the young man himself, she seemed to admire the life and work of common people almost more than that of her own class.

Especially when he rode with her to explore and enjoy the surrounding world, the stable hand was struck by her fascination with the inner life of natural things. She wasn't content with observing mere outward forms and behaviors: the way a prairie bird looked or flew, the mating songs of pond frogs or the drooping branches of willow trees. She wanted to feel the sensations of the flight of larksand the longing of creatures in mating season. Sometimes, she would make them pause for a long time so she could enter the worlds of wild creatures and their places. He had experienced some of the same attraction: not just idle curiosity, but a desire for more intimate understanding. As they shared experiences near the castle and afield, the young man realized that he was being drawn to the girl more and more. So, it was inevitable that his fascination and longing would lure the dwarf to him.

The dwarf was increasingly leaving his sleeping body behind in his cave as his dreams took him to the castle. He was present in the pigeons when the maiden tended to them, and in the docile dog when he accompanied her. And how easily he found himself embodied in her young stallion when she climbed onto the saddle and urged him to leave the corral behind for a long ride over the prairie.

It was on one of those journeys that the dwarf first felt the stable hand's loving attentions to the maiden and realized how like his own they were. Almost at once he realized that he was not just a second consciousness carried along in a body utterly different from his own. It felt as if his own adoration of the maiden was simply an enhancement of the young man's love; as if they weren't competing lovers but some mysterious union of two hearts bringing their complementary minds together in a single love.

The dwarf realized that he was merging more and more with the stable hand. He no longer found himself in his misshapen body back in his solitary cave. Even when the youth was working alone or resting in his loft the dwarf wanted to know what he was experiencing, what he felt and pondered. The young man's preoccupations with the girl were so like his own that even in the stable hand's dreams the dwarf felt them as his own.

But the dwarf had never allowed himself to imagine ever being able to find a way to directly express his adoration of the maiden, much less to somehow actually be her friend and lover. Now, in the young man's form and yearnings, the dwarf began to see a way.

All of this came to an unexpected culmination during an early morning ride one summer day. The maiden had come down to the stable, eager to be out in the forest while creatures were still in that magical transition between deep night and bright day. Nocturnal owls, whip-poorwills and prowling creatures were still active, while diurnal birds and furry creatures and reptilian life were waking. It was the richest time and the maiden loved to sense that wealth among the massive trees and little ponds.

The maiden and the stable hand sat astride their horses on a knoll, gazing down on a quiet pool. They were both absorbed in the tranquil scene: hearing the songs of small birds and the gentle croaking of waking frogs; seeing the first rays of sunlight pierce the dense canopy of surrounding trees and reflect off the calm water; smelling the pungent weeds and fragrant pollens encircling the pond; feeling the cool damp air encompass them.

The dwarf was with them in their almost mystical immersion in this magical world. But he felt no urge to identify with any particular creature to know this world from its unique perspective. Instead, it was as if he was experiencing this world in its vibrant totality as a an indescribably complex harmonious unity. If this place and time could have a single soul, it was nested in the consciousness of the dwarf. The maiden and the young man were caught up in the same mind, as if all that was present to them was within them or was inseparable from them.

Then they sensed something moving from the shadows toward the pool. It was a doe, followed by her fawn. The doe sniffed the quiet air and looked back at the wobbling fawn as they reached the water's edge. Then they both lowered their heads and began to drink. The scene was so enthralling that when the onlookers turned to face each other, their open smiles and wide eyes revealed their mutual enchantment. Both felt, more powerfully than ever before, their profound kinship.

But, before that realization could seize them, there was a sudden disturbance. The doe turned her head and immediately bolted back into the forest, with the fawn scrambling to keep up. Then a large dark wolf burst from the trees and rushed after the deer. The stable hand immediately thought to chase after the growling wolf, but before he could begin to turn his horse he realized that the maiden's stallion was panicking. He was rearing up and making a hysterical screeching sound. In an instant, his violent motions tossed the maiden off, leaving her sprawled on the ground.

The young man leaped to the ground and rushed to the maiden. When he looked into her beautiful eyes, he saw that she was stunned but conscious. She responded coherently to his concerned questions and words of comfort. Then she wrapped her arms around his neck as he embraced her. Any thought about the fleeing deer had vanished from their minds as they remained in each other's arms on the grassy knoll.

As soon as the maiden had caught her breath and was able to stand, with the young man's help, she confirmed that nothing was broken, though she felt some aches where her body had crashed onto the earth. He took her hand and led her to a large rounded rock. There they sat, still recovering from the shock of their experience and trying to regain their wonderful immersion in this tranquil world.

Gradually, their new intimacy returned as they talked about their shared sense of the sacredness of this separate world. How profound it was to enter the realm of nature this way—and to do so together. Without fully acknowledging how their friendship had been transformed in all of this, the way in which they gazed into each other and felt so free to share their understandings were clear signs that their lives could never be the same again.

The dwarf was wholly caught up in all of this. He had experienced the stable hand's bliss, alarm and shocked concern as his own. At this moment he was so completely absorbed in the intimate conversation and mutual attention of the young couple that he didn't realize how completely he had crossed over to the inmost being of the stable hand.

But, in fact, from that moment on he would never return to his remote dwelling nor revive the small misshapen creature that laid there like a hibernating beast. His old body would slowly dry up like the abandoned chrysalis of a butterfly and he would be incarnated in a form that could fully embody all that was essential to his deepest longings.

X - Love Welcomed

When the couple returned to the castle the maiden told her parents of their amazing experience. Her father and mother were assured that their beloved daughter was unhurt. They could easily see how the maiden was enthralled by what had happened and by the young man who had shared the entire event. They looked at each other with mutual awareness that something very important had changed in their daughter and that a whole array of new concerns was rising in their life. But, for the moment, they stifled their worries and were glad for their daughter's excitement and safety. After heart-felt thanks to the young man, they invited him to share their dinner.

The whole episode unsettled the relations between the stable hand and the castle's family. Now, the maiden wanted to be with the young man every day, joining him in doing his chores in the stables and gardens but also just strolling over the grounds. They were much more than servant and master: they were close friends who had shared a kind of nature mysticism and a dramatic event that had revealed an unexpected romantic attraction.

The parents were watching closely as their daughter was increasingly drawn into what was obviously a budding romance. Soon the young man was invited again to their table, something unheard of with a servant. The father cautiously inquired about the stable hand's background: where was his home? who were his parents? what were his ambitions in life?

At first, the youth was politely evasive, not wanting to reveal what he had so carefully concealed from everyone at the castle. But he understood their concerns about him, a stranger who was now their daughter's special friend. So, he told them the story of his life in Ravenwood: how he had struggled over being the only child in a prominent family, and how he had wanted to explore the world on his own to find his personal path.

That led him to tell how he had found his way to their castle and how pleased he was to be received as a peasant youth eager to learn how to work with the animals and the grounds. He went on to say, with both deference and assurance, how he had come to admire and care about their daughter. What an honor it was to improve her already excellent horsemanship and to share her deep love of their forest environment.

The young man's maturity and eloquence greatly impressed the parents and they readily believed what he had told them about his breeding and education. Now they felt secure in allowing their daughter to continue learning from him and sharing her explorations of nature with him.

In the following days and changing seasons the young pair deepened their bond, with the dwarf's constant enrichment of the stable hand's heart and mind providing a sacred depth to the youth's growing love. Often, in their exploration of the surrounding wilderness, the maiden was surprised and moved by the intuitions and empathy of her companion, especially given his sheltered village upbringing. The stable hand was also startled by his new powers of understanding creatures and their environments. He attributed this sudden sensitivity to his love of the maiden, who often seemed like a young earth spirit.

Though their deepening bond drew them away from the castle more frequently and to more remote places, they also increasingly found themselves in the company of the maiden's parents. The elders saw the couple's romantic love growing, which they wanted to keep within their observation and influence. So, the young man became a regular guest at their dinners and sometimes joined the family for evenings of music and other entertainments. By such means, the parents began to consider the possibility of the youth becoming their daughter's husband.

But, before that could be seriously pursued, they had to know much more about his family. So, using the maiden's messenger pigeons, they sent a letter to his parents, using their daughter's friend in Ravenwood as a go-between. The letter gave a brief account of who they were, where they lived, and how their son had found his way to their castle and begun a budding love relation with their daughter. The letter concluded with an invitation to visit them in the castle. An exchange of several air-borne missives resulted in the Ravenwood couple arriving at the castle in their carriage.

The parents almost immediately found each other more than acceptable, sharing many common tastes and interests. The young man's parents could easily see what a fine young woman the maiden was and how genuinely she and their son loved each other. Over a few days, the parents shared horseback tours of the nearby forests and the leisurely pleasures of a remote pastoral world. Though they dearly wanted their son to return to their village, they recognized that he wouldn't yet want to leave this new home and his beloved.

So, by the time they were preparing to return to Ravenwood, the youth's parents had begun a serious conversation about a wedding and marriage. The young couple had been reluctant to consider that possibility very realistically because of the uncertainties over their families' responses. But, as soon as they heard the elders considering their union, the floodgates of their longing burst open in a rush of loving avowals and a more intense expressions of their intimate desires.

In all of this, the dwarf was becoming even more secured in his identification with the stable hand. The longings of his own heart found expression in the words and actions of the young man. He was glad that the youth had been shaped by literature and music that enabled him to feel and articulate passions that they shared, with an eloquence and refinement that transcended anything his own rustic life had prepared him for. Though the dwarf retained his sense of a separate existence, he was so at one with the stable hand's love that there was no sense of jealousy or exclusion. Somehow, they were becoming a single lover and friend of their beautiful lady. So, the dwarf rejoiced with the young man as the wedding day approached.

XI - The Cave

Just before that festive day, the young couple set out on the longest ride they had ever taken. Their saddle bags contained everything needed for an abundant picnic. They made a little game of finding the perfect place to dismount and spread a cloth. It was so delightful that they passed up on several lovely spots, pretending to find some little fault in each so they could continue their adventure: this place was too shaded or sunny; that was too troubled with tiny insects. Wouldn't it be nicer to sit beside running water or by a sparkling pond?

Finally, they entered a region with densely wooded ravines. The slopes were lush, with large elegant ferns and cool air that flowed over them as they prepared their secret meal. Lounging beside the colorful cloth, the young lovers moved back and forth, from joking and teasing to feeding each other. Then he was kissing her fingertips and she was caressing his long soft hair. When they embraced, their mutual passion was cooled only by their promise to wait until their nuptial night to consummate their love.

As they gathered the remnants of their small feast, the young man commented on the strong force that had been leading him to ride deep into an area that was wholly new to them. The terrain and vegetation were not threatening, but there was an atmosphere of primordial life and a mysterious beauty in this place. When they heard the lush liquid song of a wood thrush flow down the ravine to them, they simultaneously turned their horses in that direction. They followed a narrow lilting stream toward its source, with the ravine narrowing around them. It felt so sheltering and safe that they began talking about the possibility of bears living nearby.

That's when they saw the dark mouth of a cave half-way up the shaded ravine wall. Just a short way past the cave, a small waterfall was spilling from a narrow opening—the origins of the stream. The couple dismounted and carefully climbed up to the cave. There seemed to be a modest path to follow, though loose rock and leaning bushes made their assent difficult. The sounds of falling water encircled them as they clamored into the little opening.

As soon as their eyes began to adjust to the darkness, they could see that the cave was a small room, just high enough for them to stand up. Even in the dim light they could make out signs of habitation near the front—a pile of empty nut shells, a gathering of twigs and moss that could have made a place to sleep or even serve to start a fire, though they saw no firepit. But who could possibly live here?

Long before that moment, when they first entered the unfamiliar region, the dwarf was overwhelmed with recollections of his home place. As the young man was engrossed in the dalliance over lunch, the dwarf had been lost in feelings and images of his solitary life. If this had happened in the past, when he was abroad in some temporary incarnation, his mind would have swept him back to this shelter and his gnomic reality. But now, even though he wanted to make that magical transformation, he felt utterly blocked. There was something outside him, alien and unknown, that presented an unbreachable wall: there was something within him, new and alluring, that held him like a powerful whirlpool, drawing him into itself.

When the young man sensed this inner ambivalence, he began to look deeper into the cave. Each moment made vision easier as they cautiously moved away from the entrance. Then the maiden made a startled gasp. She pointed to something lying on a bed of grass, curled like a sleeping animal. Because the creature didn't respond to their voices or even when they poked it with a long stick, they wondered whether it was hibernating or even dead.

But, when the youth knelt closer to examine the mysterious form, he discovered that it was some strangely human form. It was almost as small as a child, but had a rather grotesque face and head, with long coarse hair. The misshapen body was covered with an animal's pelt and its small twisted feet were bare. Whatever it was, the creature was not alive nor had been for quite a while. The young man had read about Egyptian mummies and imagined that this creature was like them, with dry leather-like skin enclosing a very small skeleton.

The stable hand carefully lifted the curled figure and carried it into the light at the cave's mouth. Now, the shaken maiden could see what her friend had described to her in the darkness. As soon as she recognized the human-like nature of the creature, she felt a wave of compassion for it. She could feel its life of isolation and complete immersion in this wild place: imagine the ways it must have fed itself by scavenging and hunting; clothed and sheltered itself; protected itself from everything that threatened it. She said it seemed like something caught between the animal and human worlds: not a welcome member of either community, but longing for acceptance in either.

As the couple talked about this creature and its plight, what it must have been like to die in such utter separation, they both felt a strong need to somehow honor him. Together, they decided to make a small excavation in the dirt floor of the cave, a dry protected grave where it could rest in peace. As they worked, their conversation drew them into a deeper sympathy with this strange being. Perhaps, just as angels are intermediaries between deities and humans, this creature was some sort of link between natural creatures and humans. Weren't they themselves beings who often felt uncomfortable in a world totally shaped by human work and purposes? Didn't they feel drawn to the natural world, apart from the preoccupations and desires of man?

As they wrapped the small curled figure in their cloth and laid him in the grave, they took turns speaking to it as a sacred being that had somehow found its place in this untouched world. They wished that there was a way to carry on his spirit in their own lives and to honor the sacredness of all natural habitats and their beautiful life.

On their long, quiet journey home, the couple talked about how to include an expression of these new commitments in their marriage vows. Their parents would somewhat understand: perhaps others would have some notion of why a young people with so much talent and fortunate circumstances would choose to live a simpler life in harmony with the wild natural world.

Through all of this, the dwarf was experiencing a deep new peace: he had found his final form and home; had realized a dream he had never clearly understood but that was now filling his whole being with inexpressible joy.

Imperial Gardens

I – The Lotus Pond

In that time, the royal line descended from Heaven and the emperor was a poet-sage. The laws were paths through the wilderness and streets in peaceful villages. Men wondered what the emperor dreamed and what he saw in his wanderings.

The emperor had many dwellings across the land—palaces and simple shelters on mountainsides, pleasure houses and domestic quarters. Each region vied to have a rarer place for the emperor, should he ever come to visit there.

In a remote region a sacred park had been kept for many years, dedicated to the emperor and awaiting his visit. The old keeper of the park had himself designed it in his youth. He had seen the park in a vision and, when he described it to authorities, they were struck by the mysterious beauty of its design. They established that the young man should be given a tract of land near a great marsh to realize his vision. His whole family was released from other labor to help in its construction.

For many years now the park had been in readiness. Secluded from the world, it was a separate universe, marvelous in every detail. Only one gate opened into it, and a single narrow path meandered among its wooded knolls, hidden grottos and lush marshlands until it arrived at a small pond in the heart of the park.

Each day the keeper walked that path, overseeing a magical world that had taken on a separate life long ago. Only the slightest alterations were needed now: the clearing of broken branches after an ice storm, the trimming of bushes that pressed too closely on the slender path, the resetting of stones tumbled by heavy rains. Otherwise, the park lived its various life freely in each season, beautiful in infinitely complementary ways. So, the keeper's walks were peaceful, like the daydreams of one recalling a golden day or awaiting a time when the longing of a lifetime is consummated.

Then, the emperor appeared, unannounced, in the region. When he learned of the park he went there immediately. The old keeper knelt before him and gave the emperor the key to the gate. The emperor removed his sandals and went barefoot down the path, the heavy gate closing behind him.

Each turn revealed new mysteries close at hand. It was at the end of summer and luxuriance was giving way to dessication, making a strange conjunction of lush flowers and drying leaves and grasses. The air was an infinite blue, unblemished by any trace of clouds, and a warm breeze rippled through the low trees. The emperor paused in a cool grotto and drank from a thin spout of water that pressed from the rocks. Slowly, he crossed the marsh on the cushioned path and came to the pond's shore.

A long slender boat rested on the landing. The emperor slipped it into the water and climbed into the boat, pushing away from the shore with the gleaming blade of the paddle. The water was dark and rolled gently under the gliding boat. Great white lotus flowers floated on the surface, their flat dark leaves making sounds like secret kisses as the waves rolled under them. The emperor let the boat drift freely into a bed of lotuses, trailing a hand in the black water until he caught the sinuous stem of one of the flowers. He felt the root tug from deep in the mud below, the stem stretching in his hand, and then it snapped just below the broad fleshy blossom. He lifted the fragrant white lotus to his face and was lost in it.

The emperor did not leave the park until the rising moon drifted on the surface of the pond. The keeper alone remained awake close by the gate and saw the emperor leave a small scroll on his doorstep. Later, in the candlelight of his hut, the keeper read the scroll:

She awaits her lord in silence;
her handmaid carefully keeps
her solitude,
her loveliness,
her sacred bond.
Desire grows from desire
to the perfection of this flower.

When he comes to take it
in his hand,
in his desire,
in his illumined mind,
the handmaid withdraws in gladness
and she is known beyond all words.

II – The Golden Fish

The royal fish keeper strolled beside his ponds one spring afternoon, resting in the beauty his family had created there over many generations. The three ponds were jewels in the brilliant light, strung together by a thread of water flowing from a spring in the hillside just above them. Each stepped pond was encircled by new grass, weeping willows and a narrow path used only by the keeper's family and by the emperor on his solitary walks.

The ponds were transparent, with dark bottoms. Golden fish floated in them like dreams, their elegant fins langorous and fragile, like silk fans. The females were suspended motionless in the clear water, thick with roe. Circling incessantly over the bottom, the males were becoming sullen and combative. Only when the keeper knelt beside the water and took pellets of food from his pocket did they change their motions, rising to pluck morsels as they touched the surface, even coming to his fingertips like little birds.

"Yes, eat, my children. Grow strong. Soon we will have clouds of fingerlings again, like bursts of golden fireworks. Don't fight, you brutes. Let my ladies come to my hand as slowly as they want. They are the bearers of it all, you crude things. We only watch over them."

In a few days the keeper would begin to separate the females, guiding them to special nests where he could oversee their breeding with the most select males. Once the veil of milt was spread over the bedded eggs the keeper would quickly remove the males. This process had gone on each spring for over a century, as his family labored to transform crude carp into exquisite golden forms. Only the finest specimens were kept — refinements of refinements, gold from mud.

The keeper stood in satisfaction beside the highest pond. He stooped to cut some watercress from the icy spring. Some of the fish nuzzled into the small cascade, as though seeking to ascend to some unknown headwaters to spawn amid snowy mountains. The keeper felt their longing.

He heard a musical twittering in the willow that leaned to the water close by him. Among the bowed branches yellow warblers were feeding and courting. The leaves were delicate, like new poems gleaming from an artist's brush. When the warblers dipped to the water, the keeper saw golden images rise to meet them. Looking out over the broad river valley, he saw the brown waters of the spring flood spreading up once more, covering the farmers' fields with silt and threatening the simple raised buildings as they did each year.

He did not realize that at that very moment an unprecedented flood was surging from the mountains. Late snow and heavy rains had loosened torrents not known before in that region. In the mountain canyons there was a roar of rolling boulders and wild water. And where the flood broke out into open country the peasants fled empty handed just to save their lives and drive their livestock to higher ground. Thus it was that in that night the flood came to the keeper's valley, reaching to the mouth of the hillside spring.

Near dawn, the keeper wakened to hear the commotion of peasants close to the royal grounds. He imagined there was a fire; but then he heard the unfamiliar sounds of water moving over the park. Descending from his loft, he found water ankle deep in his cottage. He rushed outside.

In the pale light he saw the muddy water spread over the entire valley like a lake, debris and carcasses moving ponderously on the surface. The ponds were gone, all three engulfed. The keeper's heart sank, and he wanted to disappear into the flood too. But he had to go to tell the emperor this terrible thing.

When the keeper arrived at the palace, the emperor was already issuing orders to deal with the flood. The keeper was instructed to wait in a sitting room. Finally, the emperor came. "Master, they are all lost, gone forever. The river has taken every one of them." The emperor felt his keeper's grief, knew it as his own. For it was his great delight to wander beside the ponds, contemplating until the golde fish were his very dreams, drifting in water pure as mountain air. After a long silence, the emperor said, "Keeper, let us be content with this. Your family has done a noble work, changing mud eaters into golden creatures. It is the labor of the spirit. But we are only keepers, finding what is hidden and helping it come forth." Again, a long silence. "Is it not the spawning season just now, keeper?" "Yes, excellency, and the more the pity of it." "But keeper, is not the river a most elemental thing?" They parted in silence.

Several days later, when the flood waters were receding, the emperor went down to walk by the muddy ponds. Rain had freshened the green things, but the walk was still covered with a film of slick mud. He sat on the bank by a willow and wrote a poem, which he left at the keeper's cottage.

Seeking the lowliest way,
the river joins all things.
Mountains and sea,
filth and gold,
all is borne in her.
Forms of all things
float in her waters:
seeds within seeds,
swimming up
and drifting down.

III – The Cherry Orchard

The royal family had enjoyed over a century of secure rule, allowing them to spend much of the year away from their fortified castle. In each region of the country a palace was constructed to provide access to the special features of the region: a summer palace set on a verdant plateau in front of the country's highest mountains, offering spectacular views of the snow-covered peaks and cloudless cool days to hike in alpine meadows and picnic beside roaring waterfalls; a seaside palace providing days of lazy sailing, the sounds of surf crashing on the shore, and wonderful sunset vistas that enveloped their world in golden light; and palaces that allow the family to experience the rich life and culture of their people (farming, hunting and fishing, celebrating seasonal festivals).

One of these palaces was set in the major fruit-growing region, an area favored with temperate weather and ample rain. An early emperor had dreamt of a small comfortable palace there, set among gentle rolling hills and encircled by orchards of each kind of fruit tree of that region, along with several vineyards of its best grapes. A team of master arborists and gardeners from the region was given the task of transforming the emperor's dream into a living tapestry of orchards, vineyards and gardens. Over many decades their work had created a remarkable design of fruited vegetation which, viewed from the high pavilion of the palace, offered royal observers a splendid quilt-work in all seasons.

The current emperor wanted to add his personal vision to the tapestry. That vision came to him in a dream, shortly after he had viewed a company of dancers performing for the royal family and courtiers in the castle. His dream began in darkness, with soft music murmuring like wind currents flowing through a forest. Then a full moon emerged from a dense cover of clouds, revealing a dozen ballerinas moving in concert on a grassy knoll. Each dancer was clothed in shimmering white and her hair drawn up in a bun that accentuated her elegant neck. When their dance concluded, each ballerina stood on point, slowly turning in the moonlight. Upon awakening, the emperor knew what he wanted for the orchard palace.

The very next day he travelled to the orchard region and gathered all his arborists to share his dream and gain their counsel on how to create a small grove of fruit trees to embody it. The emperor listened to their excited explorations: what fruit should it be? what place would best suit the dancing trees? When the emperor showed special interest in creating a grove of oriental cherry trees, the arborists immediately turned to practical issues of soil, sunlight, moisture, and neighboring orchard patches.

The little orchard would be set close to the palace for viewing from its pavilion. A gentle slope to the west would benefit from full sunshine during the growing season and shield the grove from the harshest winter winds. Patches of blackberries, raspberries and beds of strawberries would border the cherry trees.

But what kind of cherry trees should be planted? Some argued for ornamental but fruitless Asian cherry trees with lush double-petalled flowers that would produce luxurious white crowns each spring. Others appealed to some of the ideals which had shaped the orchards and gardens from the beginning: these should be truly 'fruitful' places, with their fruit available to the entire orchard crews, both for their family use and to be sold in the region's markets. That was the basis for the regular series of harvest festivals which ran from the earliest strawberries in May to the last firm apples in October. The cherry trees should be no exception to the historic union of beauty and utility, feeding both soul and body.

To harmonize the two possibilities, the master arborist proposed a compromise: they should introduce a new variety of cherry tree from the Orient that was renowned both for its spectacular early blossoms and for its plump dark cherries. The emperor gave his approval to this, setting the new venture in motion.

A small supply of cuttings or scions was acquired from an Eastern nursery. These were grafted to hearty local apple stock which readily accepted the foreign intruders and were soon thriving, even though it wasn't the best time of year for such work. After just one year the tiny cherry trees began putting out delicate bunches of blossoms. Within a few years the trees rose to shoulder height and bore their first fruit. The cherries were plump and ripened to a dark ruddy fullness, like sweet drops of blood.

The emperor kept a close eye on the progress of his cherry orchard, making special trips to the palace whenever the master arborist sent word of notable stages in its seasons. When an alert came that there were enough ripe cherries to be sent to the castle, the emperor rode back with the currier so he could join the first harvest himself. It pleased him so much to sit in the pavilion and gaze down on the cherry orchard as he savored its rare fruit.

After that experience, the emperor made two seasonal trips by himself to enjoy the cherry orchard: in spring, just when the trees were most resplendent in their frilly white blossoms, and in late summer, when the delicate young branches hung heavy with their gleaming succulent fruit. In spring he loved to walk at dawn among the fragrant blossoming spheres, talking to them almost as if they were his daughters during their ballet lessons. He would select a small bouquet to have close as he sat at the pavilion table taking tea. In the harvest season he would wait until the late sun had fully warmed the cherries, making the quiet air redolent with their lush ripe bodies. How he loved to gather a handful of cherries to take back to the pavilion to savor as dusk engulfed his cherished world.

There was a steady flow between the castle and the orchard palace as couriers brought news of each fruit in its season and samples of its finest produce at its peak. So, when an exceptionally early spring brought premature flowering, the chief arborist sent a courier to alert the emperor. That very day the emperor travelled to the orchard palace, riding horseback beside the courier.

Arriving in late afternoon, the emperor went directly to the hillside cherry orchard. Even with forewarning, he was startled by the radiant white spheresthat balanced atop slender dark trunks like pale balloons. He walked along the short files, talking softly to each tree as he told them how beautiful they were and how dear to him. He wasn't sure why he was so entranced by his beloved cherry trees, especially in this ephemeral fragile moment of their young lives. But he had to linger in the viewing pavilion until the full moon rose and they revealed themselves to him again. In the night, they came to him once more as the dancers who had first evoked his vision.

The next day the emperor awoke early, eager to walk among his cherry trees in the silent moist dawning. The arborist encouraged his master to use the day to tour all the other orchards, as well as the numerous gardens and vineyards that were also breaking out in premature enthusiasm. It gave him great pleasure to follow each faithful gardener as he showed the results of his lifelong labors and answered the emperor's many questions. How wonderful it was to hear the pride of each family's leader as he recollected generations of planning and work, their struggles with numerous natural challenges and their joy in serving both the royal family and the region's residents.

By late afternoon the skies were darkening and the temperature was sinking, so the emperor borrowed an arborist's jacket and went inside the palace for his dinner. Even when he walked out to the pavilion to enjoy the day's last glimpse of the cherry orchard he didn't linger long. A chill wind was rising, spattering cold rain everywhere. By daybreak most of the blossoms would likely be sprinkled over the orchard grass like a late snow shower.

But it was going to be worse than that, much worse. Weary from a day of much walking, the emperor fell into a deep dreamless sleep; so he never heard the rainfall thickening to freezing sleet. The wind dropped, but the clinging rain kept coming, covering everything with a clear coating of ice. The calm prevented branches from swaying and snapping from their unbearable weight, but with the first light of dawn the north wind began rising again. That's what brought the head arborist to the palace and then to the emperor's quarters as the butler made apologies for their disturbance.

The arborist stood close to his master's bed, holding his wet cap in both hands as he told what he never wanted to tell. "O my lord, it's so terrible. Please forgive me for interrupting your sleep and bringing such awful news. Last evening's cold rain changed to freezing rain, and then to sleet. Now all the orchards droop with gleaming ice, with many branches snapping and lying broken on the crackling ground. And what is worst of all, dear lord, your ladies, our beautiful white ladies, are all disfigured. Not a single one has escaped Nature's cruelty. Now the blossoming is suddenly done and there's no hope of a good harvest."

Later, the emperor would go out to the pavilion to gain an overview of the destruction, and would walk among the wreckage and debris of this disaster. But already his mind was filled with terrible images of this ruin and his heart ached with awful losses. He wanted to sink back into his bed and hope this was just a shocking dream. But more than that, he wanted to see for himself what was real and to take some actions that would help everyone overcome this trauma.

He stood in his nightshirt and put an arm around the arborist's shoulders. "My dear friend, you are the master of all the orchards and overseer of our many gardens. Thank you for understanding how dear our cherry orchard is to me. It is like a beautiful daughter we have together watched grow to early womanhood. We are shocked now by her unexpected disaster and cannot see hope for any magnificent recovery. But we must consider the larger circle of beauty and fruitfulness that you and so many others have within your care."

By midday the emperor had met with all the chief arborists and gardeners and was secure in their determination to go forward with all the work needed to recover from this destruction.

Before mounting his horse to return to the castle, he left a note on the chief arborist's workbench.

Watching our children dance and play,
We forget their early tribulations,
Neglect their uncertain futures.
There is only their present delight.
And our delight in them.

But this very moment
Is the fleeting fruit
Of our enduring care
And the hidden seed

Of our unending determination
To tend to them.
Thus, do they sustain us,
Even as we sustain them.

CPSIA information can be obtained
at www.ICGtesting.com
Printed in the USA
LVHW020936061121
702610LV00014B/623

9 781637 643884